THIS HOUSE WAS FREAKING HIM OUT

Alex started to hitch himself out of the pool, glancing up at the house as he did. He instantly froze in position, all his weight on his rigid arms. Something—someone—was in the downstairs window looking out at him, a pale shadow of a face above red folds of fabric. Then a white blur, like a small animal, skittered across the window ledge. He began to shiver all over as if the air had turned suddenly frigid. He worked his way along the gutter to the steps at the shallow end. But he was too shaken even to make it up the stairs. He collapsed on the second step and covered his face with his hands. Whatever was in there had been in the window by the chimney. A deep window seat flanked the fireplace . . . someone watching . . . someone dressed in red . . . This house was freaking him out.

"Judith St. George shows why the genre remains so popular in this untaxing, enjoyable chiller that plays its setting—spooky Red Roof Farm—for all it's worth . . . there are a lot of nice, creepy touches."
—*The New York Times Book Review*

Bantam Books for Young Readers
Ask your bookseller for the books you have missed

HAUNTED

BY

JUDITH ST. GEORGE

BANTAM BOOKS
TORONTO · NEW YORK · LONDON · SYDNEY

RL 6, IL AGE 11 AND UP

HAUNTED

*A Bantam Book / published by arrangement with
The Putnam Publishing Group*

PRINTING HISTORY
*Putnam edition published September 1980
Bantam edition / April 1982*

*Bantam Books are published by Bantam Books, Inc. Its trade-
mark, consisting of the words "Bantam Books" and the por-
trayal of a rooster, is Registered in U.S. Patent and Trademark
Office and in other countries. Marca Registrada. Bantam
Books, Inc., 666 Fifth Avenue, New York, New York 10103.*

PRINTED IN THE UNITED STATES OF AMERICA

0 9 8 7 6 5 4 3 2

For my sister Anne and her family

One...

It wasn't all that far from Baldwin, Massachusetts, to Wye Mills, Pennsylvania—it just seemed far. Maybe that was because Alex Phillips's father insisted on driving the whole way and he wouldn't have anything on the car radio but CBS. Absolutely no rock stations. Consequently, Alex slept almost the whole way. But even Alex, who had been known to sleep fourteen hours at a stretch, finally couldn't sleep any more.

Still, he kept his eyes closed. Maybe his father was fooled, and maybe not. At any rate, he didn't talk as Alex thought about his summer job ahead. It would be the first summer he had spent away from home since he went to camp when he was ten. Funny, back then he'd been really homesick. Now he was sixteen, he couldn't wait to get away, what with his parents on his back all the time about one thing or another—his grades, quitting his after-school job, his two car accidents, neither of which were his fault, his hassle with his track coach—and if they couldn't find anything to complain about, they manufactured it. Yes, being free and on his own for almost three months was going to be great.

Not that he was going to be completely on his own.

Bruce Buchanan, the son of Dad's best friend from law school, was sharing the job with him. Alex had been surprised and really pleased when Bruce had agreed to come. After all, Bruce was nineteen and had finished a year of college while Alex was only going to be a junior in high school. He and Bruce had been hired to house-sit Red Roof Farm, a Wye Mills estate that came complete with cars, pool, all expenses paid, plus $200 a week each. Of course the set-up was a little weird, but there had to be a catch to any job that perfect.

It was hot in the Volvo. Alex opened his eyes and reached over to turn up the air conditioner, sure that his father would automatically turn it down. It was 92° out, and the blast of cool air felt good as Alex pulled a two-week-old newspaper clipping from his pocket and read it for about the tenth time.

> Wye Mills, PA., May 30. A 72-year-old Wye Mills resident apparently shot and killed his wife yesterday morning, then killed both the family cat and himself with the same weapon, Pennsylvania State Police reported yesterday.
>
> Although Friedrich and Wilma Von Durst, locally known as the Baron and Baroness, had lived at Red Roof Farm, their 125-acre estate, for over 30 years, they were seldom seen by their neighbors and were considered reclusive by the community.
>
> Police said no suicide note was found at the scene where Mrs. Von Durst's body was discovered on the floor of the den shortly before 10 A.M. The body of her husband and their white Persian cat were found on the patio.

The investigation of the deaths is continuing.

Mr. Phillips glanced over and smiled as if Alex were a two year old clinging to a security blanket. "You're reading that article again?" he asked, predictably turning down the air conditioner.

"So what happened with the investigation, Dad?" Alex asked, ignoring the remark.

"It's pretty much been dropped. It was a definite murder-suicide. The autopsies showed the Baroness had diabetes though she wasn't really sick. But the Baron had terminal cancer. They were so totally devoted, they must have made some kind of pact."

Nobody could be that devoted. A love-death pact sounded phony, like something out of Shakespeare. But that was Dad's problem, not Alex's. Because of some old family tie from years ago, Mr. Phillips was the Von Dursts' lawyer. For complicated tax reasons, the whole estate had been in the Baroness's name and her will had left everything to the American Socialist Rights Party, whatever that was. But the new owners weren't due to take over until September and now that the guard had been taken off the house, someone was needed to protect the property for the summer. Mr. Phillips had hired Alex and Bruce to do the job.

Alex slipped the newspaper article back into his pocket and pushed his glasses back up his nose from where they had slipped down. They always slid down, just like his father's. That was because they both had long skinny noses. Though everyone said Alex and his father looked alike, Alex couldn't see it at all. Alex was thin and had a lot of thick auburn hair, and his father was paunchy and practically bald with freckles all over his pate where it got sunburned from playing tennis. Tennis was Dad's big thing, and Mom's too. In fact, after Dad dropped Alex at Red Roof Farm, he was driving to Washington for a week of business, then he and Mom planned to vacation in Virginia for a month of tennis. They could do that now that they had gotten rid of Alex for the summer and shipped thirteen-year-old daughter Julie off to camp.

"Are you sure you can handle this job, Alex?" Dad asked for the fourth time since they'd started. "You know you can't just walk out the way you did with your job at Pantry Fair."

Dad could never resist the needle about Alex quitting his job last winter. What Dad didn't understand was that the pay was terrible and none of Alex's friends was working. "I'm not going to quit, Dad. I mean, what's to house-sitting but yard work and making sure no one rips the place off?"

Besides, Bruce would be there and Alex planned to learn plenty from Bruce—about girls, about cars, about, well, just about everything. Bruce was flying into Philadelphia tonight, then driving a Hertz car from the airport to Red Roof Farm. No doubt about it. This would be the summer of a lifetime.

They were approaching a town now, bumping over railroad tracks. A gingerbread stationhouse was painted green and white and decorated with geranium-filled window boxes. "Wye Mills, PA. 17422" announced a sign on the little white post office. A hardware store, a general store, a lunchroom, a gas station and a beauty parlor made up the rest of the town.

Alex and his father drove the next few miles in silence. Rambling post-and-rail fences marked off the rolling countryside estates. Long driveways curved up to handsome houses half hidden behind stately trees and thick shrubbery. Discreet wealth was how Mom had described Wye Mills and now Alex saw what she meant.

Then, as Dad slowed down and shifted into second, Alex realized they had arrived. A wooden sign hung from the branch of an ancient apple tree by the side of the road. "Red Roof Farm." No name, no number, no street. As they turned into the driveway, for the first time Alex felt a shiver of apprehension, and he suddenly wished that Bruce were here waiting for him instead of him arriving first and waiting for Bruce. Huge oak trees met in an arc above them in a burst of early summer green, dappling the roadway with patches of shimmery sunlight. But the farther in they drove, the more tightly the trees meshed overhead until finally the drive was completely shadowed. Alex's father slowed to take a traffic bump in the road.

It was impossible to miss the sign. "Attack dogs. Proceed at your own risk. Do not leave your car. Survivors will be prosecuted."

Alex laughed. "At least the old guy had a sense of humor."

Once they were over the bump, Mr. Phillips picked up speed. "I don't think so. The Baron had a couple of Doberman pinscher guard dogs that were really vicious. Luckily the sheriff's office picked them both up, though they never did find the third dog."

"What third dog?"

"The Baron's house dog. He's been seen once or twice in the area, but no one's been able to catch him."

"No big deal if he turns up." Alex liked dogs. There wasn't a dog he'd ever known he couldn't get along with.

As Dad slowed to go over another traffic bump in the road, something to the right of the driveway winked brightly, catching Alex's attention. It was like a magnifying glass reflecting the rays of the sun. When Alex looked over, he saw an old cottage set deep in the woods, seventy-five feet or so back from the driveway. It was a gingerbready little cottage, like the Wye Mills railroad station, only it was shabby with peeling paint and a swayback roof. Sunlight must have been reflecting off one of the windows.

"What's that cottage, Dad?" Alex asked.

His father glanced over. "That old place has been on the property for years. It must have been a guest cottage at one time."

The drive curved, and the cottage disappeared from Alex's sight. They drove through deepening woods for another few minutes until, without warning, they were in a clearing with the house in full view. Alex sucked in his breath. He hadn't even thought about what the house would look like so there was no reason to be surprised. But he was. All the other Wye Mills houses they had passed had been Englishy looking brick-covered-with-ivy, or Tudor-covered-with-ivy, or field-stone-covered-with-ivy. There was nothing Englishy about Red Roof Farm and nothing farmlike about it either.

There it sat, massive and hideous, an enormous tan stucco building with a red tile roof and no ivy at all. Only overgrown clumps of dark rhododendron bushes broke its harsh lines. A long porch with a wide oak door at one end extended across the front. Windows with shades half-drawn like hooded eyes lacked even the softening touch of shutters.

Neither Alex nor his father spoke as they drove slowly around the side of the house and stopped by the back porch. The Volvo's air conditioning whirred in the silence. Unshaded and unprotected, a swimming pool a hundred feet from the house reflected a gray sky. Over to the right, at the end of the driveway, loomed a big, red-roofed barn, built of the same institutional stucco as the house. The two-acre backyard, empty of trees or shrubs, ended abruptly in a line of thick woods.

All Alex had thought about this summer was being free and on his own, plus making money and having a good time with Bruce. Now he wasn't so sure. He hadn't expected the place to look like this, to be so ugly . . . and overpowering . . . and isolated . . .

His father must have been thinking the same thing. He took off his glasses, cleaned them, put them back on, then turned to Alex with a frown. "We can get someone else to stay here with Bruce if you want, someone older, maybe."

When would his father stop treating him like a child? Alex was sixteen, had his driver's license and was almost six feet tall. "Forget it, Dad, I can manage fine."

"I'm simply saying I might not have taken everything into consideration myself. This may be a mistake after all."

The way Dad was pressing him into a corner was leaving Alex no choice. And what Alex wanted right now was a choice, to think things over, decide if he really wanted to spend his summer here, big money or no big money. Now Dad had left him no way out.

"I'm staying, Dad. Period."

Alex's voice was husky and he wasn't sure if that was from anger at his father or the tight feeling that had suddenly closed up his throat. Either way, he had to go through with it now. Reluctantly, Alex opened the car door and climbed out.

TWO...

Alex and his father stood on the back porch. They had been working for over an hour and Alex couldn't ever remember being hotter. Though it was only the middle of June, the thick air was so humid it practically dripped. A breeze stirred, but all it did was move the hot air around. Mr. Phillips took off his glasses and wiped his flushed face with his handkerchief.

"I left my hotel number in the kitchen, Alex. If you want to reach me, phone before eight in the morning or after eight at night."

Alex nodded. "No problem, Dad, and Bruce will be here soon."

Alex clung to the thought of Bruce, two inches taller then he and twenty pounds heavier.

"I checked the Mercedes, the pickup and the jeep and they all work fine. The keys are by the back door. Be sure to drive carefully." Mr. Phillips slipped Alex a $50 bill with one hand and gave him a hard hug around the shoulders with the other. "This is just an advance, son. Good-bye, and good luck."

"So long, Dad."

Alex watched his father climb into the Volvo, drive

down to the barn, U-turn, then drive past, blowing his horn and waving as he disappeared around the side of the house. Ridiculous as it was, Alex felt even worse than when he was ten and his parents had dropped him at camp.

He had a couple of hours to kill before Bruce arrived. He might as well clean the pool, then take a swim. But when Alex went in the back door, he noticed the cooler full of food his mother had packed for him. He'd better unload that first.

But the refrigerator was already stocked with food. Yuck, Von Durst food. A half-used bottle of ketchup, pickle relish, butter, cheese, V-8 Juice, a couple of rotten peaches and a brown head of lettuce. It was all more than two weeks old. The people who had bought, cooked and planned on eating this food were both dead. Shot. It was a ghoulish thought. Alex dumped everything that wasn't sealed or bottled into the wastebasket. The ketchup and other stuff he'd use later. Maybe.

As soon as Alex opened the cooler he felt better. His mother had packed all the food he liked, even a macaroni casserole with cooking directions taped to the top in her familiar scrawly handwriting. He began to unload: a canned ham, an apple pie, potato salad, even two jars of cocktail onions which he liked to eat straight. As he pushed the Von Durst containers and jars aside to make room, a bottle on the bottom shelf tipped over. He reached in to right it, then realized it was full of a milky liquid, some kind of medicine. "Insulin" read the label.

Diabetics had to take insulin every day. George Merritt in Alex's English class was a diabetic and if he didn't get his daily shot he fainted or went into a coma or something. Dad said the Baroness had been a diabetic. This must be her medicine. The insulin gave him an even more peculiar feeling than the leftover food. The Baroness needed insulin to keep her alive, but no insulin was going to keep her alive now. Alex quickly piled his food in front of it.

There, he was finished. The empty cooler would come in handy for storing beer. Though Alex had only met Bruce once, he just bet Bruce was a big beer drinker. Alex glanced at the cat clock on the wall with the swinging pendulum tail. Six o'clock. Bruce would be here in a couple of hours. It couldn't be too soon for Alex. Even in broad daylight this place was eerie. Maybe it was the silence. Total silence. Alex hadn't heard a bird, cricket, or any other normal country sound since he'd arrived.

Alex shoved the empty cooler under the table and walked through the kitchen and pantry into the dining room. He stopped, that familiar tight feeling closing up his throat. He and his father had forgotten to strip the dining room table. It was all set up for a formal dinner with a white tablecloth, wineglasses, silverware and linen napkins, just as if two people were about to sit down and eat. The white candles set in silver candelabra were half burnt down as if the Von Dursts ate by candlelight every night. What made it even stranger was that Alex knew they had no maid, cook or help of any kind, which meant they went to all this trouble themselves.

The dining room, paneled in mahogany and hung with burgundy red draperies, was terribly dark. Dad had said the original builder of the house had been a

South American mahogany dealer, which must be why all the walls were paneled with dark red mahogany wood. Even the stairs and bannister were mahogany.

Alex walked from the dining room into a living room filled with ornately carved furniture, heavy and uncomfortable looking. Gloomy oil portraits of dour-looking nineteenth century people stared down from every wall. A mirror that must have measured eight feet long by four feet high ran the length of the mantelpiece, but the pink marble fireplace was so high Alex could see himself only from the shoulders up as he walked toward the stairs.

Alex still hadn't been in the den. He just wasn't ready to face the murder site yet. Dad had been great about cleaning up the blood, and he'd taken care of it while Alex had opened windows in the rest of the house to clear the sour smell from the air. Dad had even hosed down the bloodstains out on the patio where the police had found the bodies of the Baron and the cat.

But even with the windows open, the musty odor lingered. It was so sultry, Alex wondered if the smell would ever disappear. Sweat beaded his face, a trickle of it inching down his cheek as he started up the stairs, and he knew the sweat was from more than just the heat. This place was really getting to him.

He took the stairs three at a time to get to his room at the top. It must have been a guest room. All the drawers were full of linens and sheets and blankets. And mothballs. Mothballs and dried blood made a reeking combination. At first Alex had planned to sleep in the master bedroom, but the wide fourposter bed enclosed by red curtains and the closets full of peculiar-looking red clothes had driven him back to the guest room, mothballs or no mothballs. Besides, the guest room was right at the top of the stairs.

Alex tore off his clothes, dropped them on the floor and rustled through his duffel bag until he found a pair of cut-offs. He grabbed a towel from a dresser drawer and raced back downstairs, catching a full view of himself in the mirror as he hit the landing. Alex was somehow reassured to see his long skinny legs, bony rib cage, red hair curly from the humidity, and glasses halfway down his nose. He looked the same as ever. Not that he really expected anything else, but this whole set-up was so unreal, it was almost as if anything were possible.

Alex and his father had already turned on the pool motor and carried all the equipment out of the barn. Alex picked up the long-handled strainer and started scooping out leaves and debris that had fallen into the water. Right away he noticed something in the pool. It was a dead field mouse. That was strange. It hadn't been in the pool when he and his father had turned on the motor only half an hour ago or he would have seen it. It must have fallen into the pool and drowned.

But when Alex picked it up in the strainer, he saw that the mouse's neck had been broken and it was half-eaten, as if it had been killed by another animal. Alex had seen Chuckles, his neighbor's cat, play with a mouse like that, tossing it in the air and toying with it before finishing it off. Some animal in the woods must have done the same thing with this mouse.

Alex heaved the dead mouse across the lawn, then finished cleaning and chlorinating the water. It was hot work, especially since no trees shaded the pool. Even Alex's glasses were steamed up. By the time he was done, rivulets of sweat were running down his chest. He glanced up at the sky, hoping for relief. It was soggy gray, as if the rain were massed inside the clouds, ready to burst through. But though a breeze had picked up, not a drop fell. Alex couldn't wait for it to rain. Maybe fresh air would cool things off, and more than that, clear the rotten smell from the house.

Well, he had earned his swim. Alex laid his glasses on a metal table and dove off the board into the water. It felt sluggish and warm, but at least it was cooler than the air. He swam a couple of lengths as fast as he could just to get some exercise, then rolled over and took a couple of easy lengths on his back. It wasn't much of a pool, and he'd put in so much chlorine his eyes stung, but he couldn't complain. In fact, he couldn't complain about anything. Bruce would be here soon, and Bruce would be the fresh air this place needed. And just wait until he saw that 300 CD Mercedes in the barn. Alex could picture the two of them riding around in it. Hey, why not go for a ride now to get the feel of it? Then, when Bruce arrived, he'd know how to handle it.

Alex started to hitch himself out of the pool, glancing up at the house as he did. He instantly froze in position, all his weight on his rigid arms. Something— someone—was in the downstairs window looking out at him, a pale shadow of a face above red folds of fabric. Then a white blur, like a small animal, skittered across the window ledge.

Three...

Still suspended half in and half out of the water, Alex stared at the window. Then he began to shiver all over as if the air had turned suddenly frigid. Without warning, his trembling arms gave out from under him and he sank into the pool. The water poured into his open mouth and into his lungs. Panicked, he kicked to the surface and grabbed for the gutter. Sputtering and wheezing, he clung to it as he struggled to get air past the ring of iron that bound his chest.

Alex worked his way along the gutter to the steps at the shallow end. But he was too shaken even to make it up the stairs. He collapsed on the second step and covered his face with his hands. Whatever was in there had been in the window by the chimney. A deep window seat flanked the fireplace . . . someone watching . . . someone dressed in red . . .

Of course no one was in there! This house was freaking him out. As soon as he looked again, he'd see he was wrong. But he couldn't bring himself even to raise his head. He just sat there, trying to pull himself together. Okay, he told himself, get it over with. Still breathing hard, he wiped his burning eyes with his towel and stumbled over to where he had left his glasses. He put them on. He was ready. Slowly he turned toward the house. He didn't see anyone or anything in the window at all, just something blowing in the breeze. A red drapery lined with white material was fluttering out the window.

Alex's first reaction was immense relief. His second reaction surprised him. He was angry. There *had* been something more than a drapery in that window. The impression was so clear in his mind, he couldn't shake free of it. He took off his glasses, cleaned them on his towel and put them back on. The window was empty. There was nothing to see but a curtain waving in the breeze. Alex remembered there had been no screen on that window when he had opened it. But a red drapery! He had almost had a heart attack over a red drapery? Blast all that chlorine in his eyes anyway. That, plus his nearsightedness, must have fooled him. It was a perfectly reasonable explanation. So then why did he feel all rubbery inside as if his bones had disintegrated? Alex abruptly sat down in one of the deck chairs and pulled his towel tight around his shivering shoulders.

He had no idea how long he'd been sitting there when he realized the phone was ringing inside the house. That was odd. Dad had arranged for an unlisted number so he and Bruce wouldn't be bothered by a lot of crank calls.

Trill-a-trill . . . trill-a-trill . . .

Maybe it was Dad calling. The Volvo had been acting up lately. Dad might need help. It didn't matter. Alex wasn't going in that living room for anything.

Trill-a-trill . . . trill-a-trill . . .

The phone was still ringing. Dad must really need him. Hey, wait a minute. Wasn't there a phone in the kitchen? Alex raced to the house and in the back door.

In no way did his short run justify the way his heart was beating as he grabbed the receiver off the hook. "Hello, Dad?"

"Alex? This is Jim Buchanan, Bruce's father. How are you?"

Bruce must be on his way to Philadelphia and his father was calling to confirm it. "Fine, thanks, Mr. Buchanan. Did Bruce's plane leave?"

"I've had a terrible time reaching you, Alex. Your number's unlisted. Is your father there?"

"No, Dad's gone." Alex studied the picture window by the far wall. All sorts of hanging plants and shelves of potted plants brightened that whole end of the kitchen. Alex concentrated on the plants. Somehow he knew he didn't want to hear what was coming.

Mr. Buchanan cleared his throat. "There's a problem, Alex. You know Bruce has been in Mexico for two weeks and was due to arrive here in Albany yesterday. But Bruce misunderstood and thought his job with you started next week. He's on stand-by in Mexico City, but doesn't know when he'll get out."

Alex didn't say anything. He just stared at the plants.

"Alex, are you there?"

"Yes, I'm here." He was here, all right, a million miles from the nearest neighbor, in a house that smelled of death and mothballs, with grotesque red curtains flapping out open windows.

"I'm sorry, Alex. Bruce ought to arrive by the end of the week. Can you manage alone until then?"

Alex projected a mental picture of Mr. Buchanan. Both he and Bruce were big, broad-shouldered and muscular, and they both played football. Mr. Buchanan probably still played touch football on Sundays. A house would never spook out Mr. Buchanan.

"Yeah, sure, I'm fine."

"That's the spirit. Keep in touch. Good-bye, Alex."

"Good-bye."

Alex hung up the receiver and glanced out the window. The building was L-shaped, with the pantry, kitchen and laundry room at right angles to the rest of the house. From where he stood by the sink, Alex could see right into the living room. The dark walls shone with layers of wax and rubbing. Alex's line of vision focused on a portrait of a sour old man with a goatee, and the sour looking old man's eyes seemed to be focused back on him. It was too much. He wasn't going to spend one more minute in this house.

Alex looked at the kitchen clock with the dumb cat's tail swinging back and forth. Seven o'clock. His father wouldn't be in Washington yet to reach him by phone. And his mother wasn't home. After dropping Julie at camp, she planned to tour Vermont with her sister for a week.

Alex knocked his knuckles on the windowsill as a flash of genius hit him. Why bother to phone? He'd just get on the plane, fly to Washington and go straight to Dad's hotel. He didn't care what Dad had to say about quitting his job before it began. Staying alone in this house wasn't ever part of the deal.

It would be simple. He could drive one of the Baron's cars to the Philadelphia airport, leave it in the long-term parking lot and catch the first plane to Washington. He could pay for his ticket with the $50 Dad had advanced him. All of a sudden, Alex felt better.

First he'd have to change and get his duffel bag. Alex raced through the pantry and dining room, but stopped short at the living room as a dozen pairs of eyes converged on him. He wondered if all portraits were painted with the eyes staring at the observer or just this morbid bunch.

Flip-flap. A quick motion by the fireplace set the hairs on his arms on end. It was the curtain still fluttering out the open window. That curtain would be the end of him yet. Forget it, he told himself, make a run for it and don't think about anything.

Alex charged through the living room and up to the landing in two leaps. He always was best at the sprints or anything that needed a fast start and not much stamina. He reached his room, pulled on the clothes he had just taken off, zipped up his duffel bag, and raced back down the stairs with it.

As Alex hit the bottom step, he noticed the curtain still snapping in and out. Hey, he'd have to close all these downstairs windows, especially since it looked like rain. He owed that much to the job. As he leaned over the window seat to shut the window, he noticed the red velvet cushions were covered with long white hairs. Cat hairs. They hadn't been on this window seat when he had opened the window or he would have noticed them—or had they?

He slammed the window shut. It didn't matter. He was getting out of here. Period.

Alex paused by the key rack in the back hall. There

were about fifteen keys on it, each one labeled and each one hanging on a labeled hook. Neat, neat, everything was neat. It was as if the Von Dursts had neatened everything up for death. Alex took the jeep, pickup and Mercedes keys, stuck them in his pocket, locked the back door and headed for the barn at a trot, his duffel bag bumping against his shoulder. He didn't glance back at the house. He didn't have to. He sensed it there behind him every step of the way.

Dark clouds roiled overhead, so heavy they looked ripe to split open. The wind had picked up and it was almost dark. His father had left one of the barn doors open. Alex set his shoulder against the other door and pushed it open too.

He hesitated. The barn was dark and smelled faintly of gasoline and motors and ancient horse manure. The three vehicles glowed dully in the shadows but the rear of the barn receded into blackness. A light, there must be a light. Alex fumbled for a switch and found it. A single electric bulb threw a harsh glare over the cars, but didn't begin to penetrate the far reaches of the barn. There must have once been stalls back there, but Alex wasn't about to go exploring now. The sooner he was out of here, the better.

He'd drive the pickup. Much as he'd like to take the Mercedes, he knew he shouldn't leave it in a long-term parking lot. Alex selected the pickup key from the pile, threw his duffel bag in the back and climbed in the driver's seat. He tossed the other two keys on the dashboard, inserted the key in the ignition, and turned it. Nothing. No sound at all, not even a grinding. He checked to make sure he was in neutral, then tried again. Again, nothing. The next time he pumped the gas pedal. Then he tried using no gas at all. Nothing worked. The pickup was dead. But that was strange. Dad had said all three vehicles were in good running order.

Alex climbed into the jeep. But the jeep was as dead as the pickup. Once he got a faint turnover, but as soon as he pumped the gas, it sputtered and died. Gas tank full, temperature normal, no blinking red lights. All systems go. But go where? Nowhere, that's where.

Alex got out of the jeep very, very slowly. He swallowed past the tightness in his throat. The pickup not running was one thing, but both the pickup and the jeep not running was another. He studied the Mercedes. It was a beautiful piece of machinery. And, according to his father, it ran fine. Hardly daring to breathe, he slid into the driver's seat. He didn't notice the clean smell of waxed leather, the walnut wood paneling or the sliding sun roof. All he noticed was that the Mercedes was as unresponsive as the pickup and the jeep.

The windows of the Mercedes were closed and Alex was almost exploding with the heat. But he couldn't move. The shadows of the big barn enfolded the car. It was as if he were on a safe little island surrounded by unknown seas. If he moved, he'd have to make a decision, do something, and right now his mind wasn't capable of making a decision about anything.

...Four

The heat finally got to him. He climbed out of the Mercedes, walked over to the barn doors and looked out. It had started to rain at last, not hard, but enough to agitate little circles in the swimming pool. From this angle, facing where the kitchen ell jutted off at right angles, the house looked like a massive set of shoulders tensed for action. There was no way Alex was going back in there.

That gave him two choices. One, he could spend the night here in the barn. Alex glanced back at the three vehicles. There they sat, gleaming, polished, ready to go. Yet none of them worked. All three cars out of commission were two cars too many to be a coincidence. No, he definitely wouldn't spend the night in the barn. His other choice was to walk to town. Town was a half-mile Von Durst driveway and about six miles of road. He and Dad hadn't passed many cars on the way out, but he was bound to be picked up somewhere along the way. Even if he didn't get a ride, he could make it. He was still in pretty good shape from spring track. Yes, he would walk to town.

Alex hurried back into the barn, picked up his duffel

bag and the keys from the Mercedes dashboard. He was already outside when he realized one of the keys in his hand felt different from the rest. It was. Instead of a functional black label like the others, this key holder was a carved wooden figure of a cat with green stone eyes. "Libertas" was painted across the cat in black letters. Alex couldn't imagine where it had come from. He'd certainly never seen it before. It must have been on the Mercedes dashboard all along, and he had scooped it up with the others.

He dropped the keys in his pocket and cut across the wet grass, tall now where it hadn't been cut for weeks. He had to force himself not to run as he headed past the patio and around the side of the house. If he started running, he knew he wouldn't be able to stop and he had a long way to go. It was raining harder now. His sneakers were already soaked, and his shirt was too. He lengthened his stride as he hurried down the open front driveway toward the woods. Reaching the protection of the trees was a help. Alex heard the tap-tap of rain on the heavy June leaves overhead but only an occasional drop made its way through.

He followed the driveway over the first traffic bump, then the second. All of a sudden, he remembered the little cottage by the side of the driveway he had noticed coming in. Dad had said it was once a guest cottage. Maybe there was a phone inside so he could call a taxi. He'd have to keep his eye out for it. The woods were dark now, and silent, except for the sound of rain. Dark and silent. And frightening. There was something about the way these trees formed a kind of endless tunnel that gave him claustrophobia.

Good, there was the cottage. Alex turned onto the narrow little gravel path. The place looked so run-down, he doubted there would be a phone inside, but it was worth a try. A broken wooden sign over the door said, "Libertas Cottage." But, he had the key to this cottage right in his pocket! He pulled it out. There was too little light to read the tiny lettering on the cat label, but he remembered the word "Libertas." Alex had taken one hated year of Latin before dropping it forever. "Libertas" meant liberty or freedom or some such thing in Latin. He inserted the key in the lock and opened the door.

Right away Alex smelled a powerful mixture of smells in the stuffy room: paint, turps, stale cigarette smoke, but mostly cat. He ran his hand along the wall searching for a light switch. Click. Two lamps blinked on. The outside of the cottage was so shabby, the inside was a surprise. It was just one big room, brightly decorated in yellow and orange and filled with deep comfortable looking chairs and a long sofa with the cushions still squashed down as if someone had just gotten up. The far side of the room was all windows, with the sills crammed with house plants. Hanging plants and shelves of plants filled the whole space.

An artist must work here. A half-finished picture on an easel was set up by the windows and the walls were covered with bright crazy looking paintings. Rags and brushes and tubes of paint were scattered all over as if the artist were due back any minute.

Alex didn't see a phone anywhere, but all of a sudden he was too tired and wet to care. He'd spend the night here and if the artist came back, he'd just explain who he was. After all, the cottage was on Von Durst property, and Alex had been hired to caretake the whole estate.

He worked the stiffness out of his shoulders where they ached from carrying the duffel bag, peeled off his wet clothes and got a dry change from his bag. There, he felt better.

First things first. Get rid of that smelly cat litter box he had spotted over by the fireplace. And the ashtrays too. They were filled to overflowing with butts. Trying not to breathe in, Alex carried the litter box and the ashtrays outside and left them on the front porch. Next, open the windows. Alex was glad they had screens. Moths and insects beat against them frantically to get at the light inside. He had to move a big purple plant to reach the windows. With its strange, ruffled, waxy leaves, he had never seen a plant like it.

Two doors led off the main room. The first was a closet crammed with artist's gear, canvases, dried-out paint tubes, beat-up sneakers and a couple of smocks covered with paint. The clothes were small enough to belong to a child. Alex had guessed the artist was a man, but now he realized it must be a woman, a very small woman.

The other door opened onto what Alex was looking for, a bathroom. He cleaned up and got ready for bed. Luckily, the sofa was long enough to take his whole length. As he arranged a blanket under his head, he noticed a big painting on the wall above the sofa. It was a picture of some kind of big bird soaring over a wide canyon with mountains in the distance. Neither the forms nor the colors were traditional, but he liked the free, open sweep of it.

Alex reached behind him and turned off the light. He was totally and completely beat. But sleep wouldn't come. Though he kept turning over, trying to find a more comfortable position, it didn't work. He just couldn't fall asleep. His thoughts kept revolving around and around. To the dead mouse in the pool . . . to the drapery in the window that had looked so lifelike . . . to the white cat hairs on the window seat . . . the cars that wouldn't start . . . having the key to this cottage just appear in his hand. Taken alone, none of those things was anything special, but put altogether, they were unexplainable . . . bizarre . . .

Alex must have fallen asleep at some point because he dreamed about his old dog Wendy who had died last year at fourteen. He even heard the tinkling of her license and name plates as she came running in answer to his whistle. His dreams were so real, when he woke up, he looked down expecting to see Wendy sleeping beside him the way she used to. But there was nothing to see but rippled sunlight patterning the rag rug and nothing to hear but the shrill chorus of birds in the woods. Saddened by his dream, Alex rolled over and tried to go back to sleep. But the cottage was flooded with morning light and it was hopeless. He reached for his glasses on the floor, put them on and held his wrist-watch up to his face. 6:10.

His stomach growled with hunger and he suddenly realized one reason he couldn't get back to sleep was because he hadn't eaten since yesterday noon and he was famished. His stomach growled again and when he stood up he felt lightheaded. If only this cottage had a kitchen. Whew, he'd never make it all the way into town, and at this unreal hour, there probably wouldn't even be cars on the road to pick him up.

He considered alternatives to walking. He could go back in the house and get something to eat, or he could try the Baron's cars again. Last night's rain had cleared the humidity from the air, and it was a beautiful June day. Maybe, just maybe, one of those cars would work this morning. Last night he had been frantic, pumping the gas, working the clutch, shifting, turning the key in the ignition over and over. And probably the motors had been damp. Considering how hungry he was, the cars were certainly worth a try.

Alex locked the cottage door behind him and headed back up the driveway. It was a ridiculously perfect Disneyland kind of day with the trees reflecting silver in the clear puddles. Alex avoided looking at the house when he reached the clearing. Instead, he followed the same route he'd taken last night through the wet grass, around the side of the house, past the patio and down to the barn. Wow, he had left both barn doors open. He really had been rattled.

Alex held onto the roll bar and swung into the jeep. He inserted the key, and with his foot on the clutch, gently gave it gas. The motor turned right over. He was so astounded, he yanked his foot off the clutch without thinking and the jeep lurched to a stall. Afraid he had blown his one chance, he tried again. It started right up again, trembling beneath him like a horse at the starting gate. He shifted into first and maneuvered past the Mercedes out the wide barn doors.

Hardly able to believe his good luck, he braked and checked over the dashboard. All systems were in working order. He shifted into first again and started up the driveway. As he swung around the side of the house and passed the long front porch, he shifted smoothly into second. But it wasn't until he entered the dark canopy of woods that he realized he was really on his way, to town, to Philadelphia, anywhere he wanted to go. He was free. Free! He had panicked last night over nothing. Why, he bet the pickup and the Mercedes ran fine this morning too.

Alex honked the horn out of sheer joy. At the harsh beep, the trees came alive with birds, chattering and squawking as they flew out of his way.

Five...

The first thing Alex noticed when he reached the end of the driveway and turned right toward town was a handsome white house across the way that nestled neatly into the landscape. It looked sleepy, as if no one were awake yet. On the crest of a hill, two riders on horseback were outlined against the brightening sky. A gray pickup truck clattered past going in the opposite direction and the driver waved as he passed. All of a sudden, Alex felt good, really good. He was part of the human race again. Everyone was going about normal everyday business on a sunny spring morning. The shadows and gloom of Red Roof Farm were all behind him.

Because the road was empty, Alex picked up speed. He had never driven a jeep before and was surprised at how hard it rode. He'd hate to go any farther in it than the Philadelphia airport. Thinking of the airport reminded him of his father. Was he glad he hadn't phoned Dad last night. He had been so freaked out he might have said anything, and that would have given Dad the opportunity to raise his old "I told you so" flag.

Alex slowed down as he approached town. First to

the garage for gas and directions to the airport. But Duffy's Garage was locked up tight. In fact, everything in town was closed except a store that had a hand-painted sign over the door: "Osborne's, 7 A.M. to 9 P.M." Alex pulled up opposite the big front window and parked. It wasn't seven yet, but the door was open, and if he had to wait one more minute to eat he was going to pass out. A little bell tinkled overhead as he went in. Right away he smelled coffee, but he didn't see anyone.

"Hello?" he called.

Over in the far corner of the store, a girl's head popped up. She must have been bending over one of the shelves.

"Hi," she replied and stood up.

Things were looking up. She was a tall, thin blonde and Alex had always liked blondes. She was almost his height, which meant she must have been at least five feet ten. As she walked toward Alex, he checked to see if she were wearing heels or clogs, but all she had on was sneakers. In the checking, he noticed she wore cut-off jeans and had great legs.

Alex grinned. "Can I get a cup of coffee and some doughnuts?"

She smiled back and Alex saw her teeth were separated just a little in the front with a tiny chip off the corner of one. "I don't know if the coffee's done yet," she said in a flat kind of accent that Alex couldn't place.

A door slammed in the back and another girl came in. She was shorter than the first girl and older, with shiny black hair and lots of eye makeup. She was pretty in a plastic sort of way. Actually, what Alex noticed first was that she wore a halter and shorts and had a fantastic build.

She barely glanced at Alex. "We're not open yet," she snapped.

"Your door was unlocked. I just wanted some coffee."

"Oh well, all right." The girl sounded annoyed. She looked annoyed too, as she poured a styrofoam cup full of coffee and pushed it across the counter.

"Cream and sugar, please, and two doughnuts." There was a pile of stale-looking honey doughnuts in the case, but the black-haired girl only yawned as she walked over to the front window and looked out as if she hadn't heard him. She pulled a pack of cigarettes from her pocket and lit up. Alex flushed red at the brushoff, not knowing quite how to handle it. He couldn't drink coffee without something in it.

The tall blonde girl must have seen him blush. She looked embarrassed, too, as she found some cream in the refrigerator and passed it over the counter along with the sugar bowl and the doughnuts. He took the coffee, poured in the cream and threw in three teaspoons of sugar. He didn't say anything as he gave the tall girl a $5 bill and waited for change.

"Hey, is that your jeep?" The girl at the front of the store rapped on the window to indicate his jeep outside.

"Yeah, at least for the summer."

"What do you mean? Are you working at Red Roof Farm?" The girl's voice was practically a shriek.

"I'm caretaker for the summer." Alex had forgotten that "Red Roof Farm" was painted on the jeep doors.

The black-haired girl hurried over to where Alex stood eating his doughnut. Her face was animated with excitement. "You're kidding," she cried. "You are kidding! I don't believe it. You're taking care of the house where they had all those murders?"

"Sure, why not?" Alex was beginning to feel a little more confident.

"I have been wanting to see that place so bad. I mean, that couple were the town mystery anyways, then with those killings, it's all people have talked about for weeks."

The girl stubbed out her cigarette and moved closer. Her perfume was musky-strong and Alex backed up a step. "How did you get the job?" she demanded.

"My father was the Von Dursts' lawyer." Not that it was any of her business.

The black-haired girl lifted the top off the doughnut case and handed Alex another doughnut like a bribe. "I'm Sherrie Osborne, and this is my cousin from Milwaukee visiting for the summer. What was the house like? I mean, was there blood all over the place?"

Though Cousin-from-Milwaukee acknowledged the introduction with a nod, Alex still didn't know her name. At least he identified the accent as midwestern. "I'm Alex Phillips." He introduced himself directly to Cousin, hoping to get her name in return.

The tall girl obliged. "I'm Joanna Hebbel." Unexpectedly she put out her hand. But Alex was caught with a coffee cup in one hand and a doughnut in the other. He quickly put down his cup, spilling the hot coffee on the counter as he returned Joanna's handshake. Close up, he noticed that faint freckles covered her nose. She looked about sixteen, Alex's age, or maybe older. "I've never been east before," she said. "This part of Pennsylvania is beautiful."

"Actually I don't live around here either. I live north of Bos—"

"Isn't there a pool at Red Roof Farm?" Sherrie interrupted. "Joanna and me would love to come out for a swim. Practically everyone in Wye Mills has their own pool but us. I mean, Dad just owns this store and works part time at the plant, so we aren't exactly in the pool class, you know what I mean?" Sherrie's voice, pitched high to begin with, was getting shriller.

"I guess it would be okay," Alex answered.

As a matter of fact, why not? Alex had never heard any rules that girls couldn't come out for a swim. Yeah, when Bruce arrived, they'd ask both girls out, maybe even have a cookout. All sorts of possibilities began to open up.

"How about today?" Sherrie pressed. "Dad believes in slave labor so Joanna and me are stuck here every afternoon until four, but we could come out after work."

Right away Alex knew he'd gotten in over his head. Entertaining two girls, one who was older for sure and one maybe older, was more than he could handle. No, he'd better wait until Bruce arrived.

"Today's not so good." He tried to play it cool. "I have some things to clean up, but give me your phone number and I'll call when everything's in shape, maybe the end of the week." There, let them think there was lots of blood to mop up.

Alex was already in the jeep on his way back to Red

Roof Farm before he remembered he had planned to ask for directions to the Philadelphia airport so he could fly to Washington. The sun shone down on him as he bumped along. Alex thought of Joanna's blonde hair pulled back in a ponytail and her hazel-brown eyes and nice handshake. She certainly wasn't beautiful, but she was okay. All of a sudden the summer stretched invitingly ahead. Maybe he could manage to stay alone at Red Roof Farm until Bruce arrived after all. He could sleep in the guest cottage at night and stick to the kitchen for meals during the day. And if he could hack that, it meant he didn't have to crawl back to Dad with his tail between his legs. Besides, it wasn't as if he were trapped here. Now that he was sure the jeep worked fine, he could leave any time he wanted.

Six...

Alex spent the rest of the morning mowing the lawn. The grass was heavy and wet, but the mower was oiled and in perfect running order. Having no trees in the yard made the job easier, but the sun was surprisingly hot and the mosquitoes had multiplied by the millions during last night's rain. By noon Alex was covered with red welts, but the compost pile of mowed grass out by the empty dog kennels was two feet high.

Alex stripped and dove into the pool. The little grass clippings that clung to his sticky skin floated to the surface. As he swam a dozen lengths or so, he made a special effort not to glance at the house, not once. He wasn't about to be fooled by his no-glasses myopia a second time.

A half hour in the pool and Alex had worked up a real appetite. I won't go beyond the pantry, he promised himself as he unlocked the back door. The big old-fashioned kitchen was cheerfully sunny. It must be all those plants by the window, Alex decided, as he walked over to inspect them. His mother had lots of house plants too, but none of them looked as good as these. That was strange. Here was another one of those waxy, purple-leaved plants like the one in the guest cottage. He had never seen a plant like this before and now he'd seen two in two days. Hey, he suddenly realized, these plants were his responsibility like the rest of the place. He'd better water them right away.

Alex filled the watering can. But as he watered a big hanging spider plant, the water leaked right out the bottom and dripped all over the floor. He reached up and felt the soil. It was wet. He checked a couple of the other plants. They were all damp too, as if they had been recently watered. Dad must have taken care of them yesterday. That was okay with Alex. He'd forget the plants and start in on lunch.

Alex opened the refrigerator and pulled out the ham, cheese, bread and milk his mother had packed. He took a long drink of milk from the carton. There wasn't much left. He should have bought more at Sherrie's store today along with some 6-12 for the mosquitoes. Sherrie. She wasn't his type. He never knew what to say to girls like that who came on strong. He liked quiet girls like Joanna who didn't expect a guy to be witty. Alex found himself thinking a whole lot about Joanna as he made two big sandwiches and ate them.

He yawned, stretched, and glanced at the clock. It was almost two. The Boston Red Sox were playing the Yankees today in Yankee Stadium, starting right now. Alex knew there was a color TV in the den. He had resolved not to go beyond the pantry, but seeing that game was awfully tempting. Alex had been a Red Sox fan forever and never missed a game in Fenway Park if he could help it, even when it meant cutting school. And here he was doing nothing, with a TV available and waiting for him. It was ridiculous to miss the game just because he'd scared himself witless last night.

Alex paused at the dining room door. Even on a perfect June day like this, the paneled and draperied dining room glowered darkly red. And he still hadn't cleared off that table yet. Without looking left or right, he hurried through the dining room, then the living room, refusing to let any of the portraits' mesmerizing eyes catch him up short.

The den was as dark as the rest of the downstairs. It was the first time Alex had been in it. Without meaning to, Alex glanced at the desk. It was where the Baroness had been sitting when she was killed. Alex's eyes involuntarily traveled from the desk to the jagged bullet hole in the mahogany paneling, and from there down to the damp stain on the rug where Dad had tried to clean up the blood.

The baseball game, get on with the game and forget the blood. Alex turned on the TV. It was instant color and perfectly tuned. Alex was sure the Baron wouldn't tolerate anything else. The Yankees were already lined up and the Red Sox players were being introduced. Each had his own mannerism; hitching up his pants, chewing tobacco, a big grin, a certain way of walking. It was like watching old friends come into the room. Alex sat down in the big leather chair that was just the right distance away from the set. It felt coolly sticky on his bare back. He realized with a start it was probably the Baron's chair. As the stadium organ swung into "The Star Spangled Banner," he moved to a smaller, not so comfortable chair.

The game got off to a bad start. The Red Sox were

terrible, with errors, spills, bad pitching and worse hitting. By the end of the fourth inning, the Yankees were ahead 4–1. It was so painful, Alex's attention began to wander. From where he sat he could see the portraits that hung on the living room walls, frowning, stern, judgmental faces. He wondered if any of them were portraits of the Von Dursts. Probably not. The clothes were too old-fashioned. Come to think of it, he had no idea what the Von Dursts looked like, though he pictured the Baron with a walrus mustache and a monocle, and the Baroness as tall and bony with steely gray eyes.

Now Alex's curiosity was aroused. Maybe there were photographs of the Von Dursts somewhere. Certainly there weren't any in view around the house. He got up and walked over to the leaded glass doors of the floor-to-ceiling bookcases. As soon as he opened one set of doors, he saw that all the books were in a foreign language. German, he supposed.

The second pair of glass doors opened onto more books, but this time Alex saw that the two top shelves were photograph albums, arranged by date. He took down the first album, 1911–1915. It was of crumbly leather and filled with faded brown-and-white photographs, with handwritten foreign-language descriptions in white ink that were probably German too. Certainly the photographs looked German, with huge, stone castles and people dressed in strange clothes beside foreign-looking cars. These must be pictures of the Baron's family. Or maybe the Baroness's.

Alex checked over the rest of the albums. Eight years of albums were missing, from 1937–1945. Those were

World War II years. Probably the Baron was off fighting somewhere for Germany and Der Fuehrer. Alex replaced the old album and took down the album for 1949.

Now he was getting somewhere. The black-and-white pictures were of Red Roof Farm, not Red Roof Farm as it was now, but run-down and shabby, with the yard overgrown with scrub trees and weeds. But there was no mistaking the house. It was even uglier set in the clutter and undergrowth of 1949 than it was now.

And that must be the Baron and Baroness standing by the barn. Of all things, a German shepherd dog stood between them. That the Baron would own Doberman pinschers for guard dogs and a German shepherd for a pet was so in character, Alex almost laughed out loud. "F. and W. and Klaus" read the inscription under the picture. Klaus must be the dog because Alex knew the Von Dursts' first names were Friedrich and Wilma. Neither of them looked anything like he had imagined. The Baron was tall and thin, with jug ears and a receding hairline, and neither a mustache nor a monocle. The Baroness was more than a foot shorter than her husband, so either he was terribly tall or she was terribly short. Probably both, Alex decided. She looked thin in her summer dress, though he noticed she had heavy upper arms and thick ankles as if maybe she'd once been fat and had lost a lot of weight. They both looked about forty or so, though Alex wasn't a very good judge of age.

A roar went up from the TV and Alex rushed over. A ball was sailing into the stands, a Yankee ball. Disgusted, Alex watched the Yankee runners lope around the bases. What a disaster of a game. He put the 1949 album back and took out the newest one, spring of this year.

It was full of color pictures, neatly organized and labeled like the rest. He flipped through it. The Baron was gaunt and lined now, with only a fringe of white hair, and the Baroness seemed smaller and thinner than ever. Though the Baron was smiling in most of his pictures, the Baroness had a peculiar, vacant expression. In almost every picture, the Baron had a German shepherd with him. "Klaus" said the label. It gave Alex a start until he realized it couldn't be the same Klaus of over thirty years ago. It must be a different dog with the same name.

Both the Baron and Baroness wore red in almost every picture, a red jacket, red evening dress, red bathing robe, red slacks. Alex wasn't surprised. He had seen those very costumes upstairs in the master-bedroom closet. What interested him more was a big medallion the Baroness wore around her neck in all her photographs. It looked vaguely familiar, but the room was too dark to see clearly and the flickering light from the TV didn't help.

Alex glanced at the screen as the score flashed on. Yankees 7, Red Sox 1. He obviously wasn't missing much. He carried the album over to the window and pulled the drapery back. As soon as his eyes adjusted to the bright light, he studied the medallion in one of the pictures. It was the metal figure of a cat with bright green eyes. Why, it looked like the same kind of cat as the one carved on the wooden key label for Libertas

Cottage. He pulled the key ring from his pocket and compared them. They *were* the same.

Alex slowly walked back to his chair to watch the rest of the game, but it was hard to concentrate. Not only was the game going from bad to worse, but his mind was stuck like a broken record on that cat medallion. Still, why should he be surprised that the Baroness's cat medallion and the key label were alike? After all, the cottage was on Von Durst property. Maybe the artist was the Baroness herself. No, that couldn't be. Nothing about those free, crazy paintings fit the woman in the albums with her strange red costumes and deadpan expression. And the warm, messy cottage couldn't have been decorated by the same person who lived in this great, glum house with its heavy, dark furniture and straightened-up-for-death neatness.

Alex forced himself to watch the whole ball game, but he would have been hard put to know what the score was at the end of it. As soon as it was over, he closed up the house and casually strolled toward the cottage, casually because he didn't want to admit even to himself how important it was to him to find out if Libertas Cottage belonged to the Baroness or not.

It did. As soon as Alex studied the paintings up close, he realized they were signed in the corner—not by a signature, but by the figure of a Roman-looking cat that was identical to the medallion and the key label. That meant not only was this the Baroness's cottage, but the Baroness was the artist. He looked at the half-finished painting on the easel. She must have been working, put down her paints and left, probably expecting to come right back. He remembered how the sofa cushions had been crushed as if someone had just gotten up from them. It was as if the Baroness had left the cottage in a hurry and were planning to return shortly. Instead, she had been killed by her husband. It was a pretty heavy thought.

Quickly Alex straightened up the cottage. At least he piled up the magazines and stuffed all the painting equipment in the closet out of sight. He just couldn't stand to have the place look like the Baroness were about to walk in the front door and pick up where she had left off.

But as he scooped up the paint rags from the floor, he happened to notice the shelves of blooming plants. They were just like the plants in the kitchen of the big house. In fact, the two purple-leaved plants were identical. Alex stared at the plants for a long time. Then slowly, reluctantly, he put out his hand and touched the soil in first one plant, then another, until he had checked every one. They were all the same. Damp and freshly watered.

Seven...

Alex had a really hard time getting to sleep that night. There was no way his father could have watered those plants. And Alex certainly hadn't. A caretaker, a cleaning woman, a friend had taken care of them. But it wasn't that simple. The Von Dursts didn't have a caretaker, a cleaning woman, or as far as Alex could tell, a friend either.

Alex drifted in and out of sleep for hours. Then all of a sudden, he was totally awake. Moonlight streaked the room with silvery patterns. His immediate reaction was that Wendy had gotten out and was barking to come in. But as he reached for his glasses, he realized it wasn't Wendy he heard. Somewhere in the woods a live dog was barking, and it wasn't the sound of a dog demanding to be let in. It was the steady, monotonous barking of a dog that had treed an animal.

Alex tried to ignore it. He had no intention of poking around the woods at this hour after some dog. He lay down again and closed his eyes. Finally, with the barking still echoing in his head, he dozed off.

When he woke up, the room was radiant with light, not the thin light of moonbeams, but the heavy gold of sunshine. Alex had fallen asleep with his glasses on. He pushed them back up his nose and checked his watch. 6:10. 6:10 was getting to be a habit. As he groaned and sat up, he remembered the dog. Dad had said the Baron's house dog was still loose. Klaus, that was the name of the German shepherd in the photographs. Alex hadn't owned a dog since Wendy died, and the idea of having a dog appealed to him. A dog would be solid and dependable and predictable when everything else around here was so unpredictable.

Alex stood on the front porch. "Here, Klaus. Here, Klaus. Come, boy," he called, not certain at all if the dog he had heard in the night was Klaus or not.

But there was no response other than the angry chatter of a pair of bluejays. Alex was already across the little porch and down the rickety stairs to check the woods behind the cottage when he noticed the dog tracks. They sank deep in the damp ground. Alex hunkered down to get a better look. It wasn't just one set of tracks, but many.

Puzzled, Alex stood up and followed them. They circled the cottage, around and around. Alex felt sure they were the tracks of only one dog, or they would have been side by side, or at least more rambling. These prints were like a path, one set on top of another as if the dog were patrolling the cottage. And the tracks had to be new. The recent rain would have washed any old tracks away.

All of a sudden, searching the woods didn't seem like such a good idea. They stretched endlessly dark at this hour, overgrown and damp. Without verbalizing even to himself why he did it, Alex reached down and picked up a good strong stick. He snapped off the smaller end twigs and whipped it through the air, reassured by its sturdy length.

Alex kept a sharp watch out on both sides of the driveway as he headed for the house. For some reason he felt uneasy, which wasn't like him. He had never been afraid of a dog in his life. But he didn't see or hear a dog the whole way. That had probably been just a neighborhood stray out there last night after all. Alex climbed the back steps and let himself in the house.

His shrugging off the whole incident was what made the sight of the dog all the more startling when he came down the back porch stairs after breakfast. The dog was just lying on the grass as if he were waiting for Alex. It was a big, wide-chested German shepherd, brown and black, with almond-shaped yellow eyes slit to a streak of light. Klaus.

A deep growl started in the dog's chest as he rose to his feet, his tail up. His hackles lifted, full and thick, visibly bristling. Then he lowered his head and shook it. His license and name tags tinkled and, as Alex stared into those yellow eyes, he realized that was the tinkling sound he had heard in his sleep, not just last night, but the night before too, when he had dreamt of Wendy.

Alex put out his hands palm side up to show he had nothing in them. "Good Klaus. Good boy."

Alex knew immediately by the way the dog's ears pricked up at his name that this was indeed Klaus. Then the dog growled again, not from his chest this time, but from somewhere deep in his gut. If Alex had a ruff of fur around his throat, it would have bristled too, only his would be from fear. There was no way this dog wanted to be friends or would even consider it. He started advancing toward Alex, one deliberate step at a time, but now his ears lay flat against his head and his eyes bored into Alex's. Instinctively Alex took a step back, though he knew it was the worst move he could make. He glanced quickly around for a branch or anything to use for a weapon, but saw nothing. Like an idiot, he'd left his stick in the kitchen.

"Good Klaus . . . good Klaus . . ." Alex murmured, continuing to back up as Klaus advanced on stiff legs, his tail rising. He bared long teeth and snarled. Beads of sweat moistened Alex's upper lip like a mustache. Then without warning, the dog's ears went up and he started wagging his tail. Almost indifferently, he turned away from Alex and walked back to where he had been lying before. He stretched out, rested his head on his forelegs and half closed his eyes as if he were dozing.

It was astounding. Alex certainly hadn't done anything to make Klaus retreat like that. In fact, Alex's obvious fear and the way he had backed off were probably the two things guaranteed to incite an attack. It was as if someone had snapped his fingers and ordered the dog to withdraw.

Keeping an eye on Klaus, Alex ran up the back stairs and into the house. He filled a soup bowl full of water, found some dog food in the pantry, picked up his stick and went back outside. Klaus hadn't stirred. Cautiously, Alex went back down the stairs and placed the food and water in plain sight. Still Klaus didn't move.

Alex circled slowly around him. The dog's thick coat was matted with briars and leaves and twigs. He must have been living in the woods these past weeks, eating rabbits or birds or whatever small game he could catch. Alex remembered how Klaus had barked last night as if he'd treed an animal. Wendy used to tree the neighbor's cat and bark on and on like that. Maybe Klaus had treed a cat. The Von Dursts' white Persian cat. What a stupid idea! The Von Dursts' white Persian cat was dead, shot and killed by the Baron right over there on the patio. Whew, he'd better cool it.

Because it was still too early to drive into town to buy supplies, Alex cleaned out the pool and finished up the mowing. The whole time he was working, Klaus watched with his flat amber eyes from where he lay by the back porch. He only moved once, and that was to get up and sniff the food and water, then walk away without touching it as if to show his disdain.

For the first hour or two that he worked, Alex was really uptight about Klaus. But after that, when he saw the dog wasn't going to move, he began to get accustomed to the still figure. Alex was sweaty and hot as he gathered up the last of the grass clippings. Yesterday's beautiful weather had dissipated into a humidity that must have been about 98 percent, and the mosquitoes were out in full force. A low gray sky pressed down as the sun steamed rather than burned him. Alex had stripped to his shorts, and he was covered with bites and scratches. He'd better shower in the house when he was finished. He planned to stop and see Joanna and Sherrie, and a swim in the pool wouldn't do the trick. He needed soap and hot water.

As Alex pushed the last wheelbarrow of clippings down the driveway toward the compost pile behind the barn, he didn't notice the sound behind him. At least not at first. Then slowly, it permeated his whole being, even before his ears relayed the message to his brain. Though the air was suffocatingly still, it was hard to tell where the noise was coming from. All he knew was that a shudder of goose bumps ran up his back at the faint tinkling sound. Klaus. Klaus was behind him, his license and name tags jingling and his nails clicking on the macadam driveway. Alex didn't dare stop. He didn't dare change his pace. Least of all, he didn't dare turn around. The sound was louder now, coming nearer, not hurrying, but closing the gap between them in a leisurely way.

It was as if fear dried Alex right up. His body, his throat, his mouth were instantly dry. It was even hard to put one foot in front of the other, as though his bones and sinew and muscle had dried up too. Alex knew he was releasing such a powerful aroma of fear he could almost smell it himself, but he couldn't help it. And he had to keep going. He bumped the wheelbarrow over the driveway onto the grass. Now the squeak of the rubber wheel was muffled. The dog must be walking on the grass too. The tap of his nails was silenced, but behind Alex the clinking of his metal tags was as loud as clanging cymbals.

Eight...

Alex kept going, pushing the stupid wheelbarrow as if it were the most important thing in the world. Now he was past the closed barn doors and still no solution came to him. He wanted to swallow but his mouth was too dry even to work up spit. The jingle of the metal tags was right at his heels now, and he didn't have to turn around to see that powerful chest and those narrowed eyes. Then he was behind the barn approaching the compost pile. Vaguely he noticed the wire expanse of empty dog cages.

There was nothing vague about the fierce rumble that started in the bowels of the dog and ended in a sharp bark of attack. Alex spun around in time to see Klaus hurl through the air toward him, his lips curled back showing his full length of teeth. Hardly aware of what he was doing, Alex tipped over the wheelbarrow with one quick motion. It crashed between the dog and him, grazing Klaus's outstretched belly just enough to deflect his charge. Klaus crashed against the wire fencing a foot beyond Alex and fell to the ground in a blur of sharp yellow teeth and thick saliva.

The second Klaus hit the ground, he righted himself

and wheeled for another attack. His fur was lifted the length of his back, from his head to his tail. Terrified, Alex flattened himself against the wire fencing. The wires moved under his hands. There was a door behind him and the door was unlocked! Alex pulled it toward him and half slid, half fell inside the dog cage as Klaus sprang again with a howl of rage. Alex yanked the wire door shut and held it shut with all his strength as the dog's body landed full force on the wires.

Unfortunately, the door latched from the outside, and Alex's fingers were so shaky he could barely squeeze them through the wire to slip the hook into the catch. Then, just as he got the lock fastened, the dog leaped again, hitting the door with such fury he ricocheted off the wires and crashed to the ground.

The cages had been built onto the rear wall of the barn. Dazed, Alex backed up against the rough stucco. He was locked inside the dog cage and the dog was on the outside. The reversal of their positions somehow confused him. And he was cold and shivering. He must be in shock. But he couldn't be in shock. He had to think straight. Already Klaus had regained his balance and was pacing up and down outside the door.

Alex was safe for the time being, safe but trapped. He remembered how Klaus had patrolled the cottage last night and knew the dog would never give up his vigil. Back and forth, back and forth Klaus paced. This kind of dog behavior was understandable. What wasn't understandable was why Klaus had lain motionless for over two hours, then, without provocation, attacked. Dogs just didn't behave that way unless there was a reason, especially a disciplined dog like Klaus. Something had triggered him. Alex didn't think it had been he. No, he had ignored Klaus completely for at least an hour before the attack. It was more as if the dog had been acting under some kind of command or signal.

But Alex was wasting his time trying to figure it out. He had to get hold of himself and think of a way out or he'd rot in here forever. He studied the situation. He was in the first of two adjoining cages. This must have been where the Baron kept his two Doberman pinschers. If Klaus were the Baron's harmless family pet, Alex hated to think what those Dobermans must have been like. The two cages were connected by a swinging gate that was about two feet wide and two feet high. It looked just big enough for him to squeeze through. Good, there was a latch on the second cage door too. Maybe, just maybe, he could fool Klaus, though somehow he sensed Klaus wasn't going to be easy to fool. Still, it was worth a try.

As Alex crawled through the connecting gate into the second cage, Klaus ran around to stand guard outside that cage door just the way Alex had anticipated he would. Quickly Alex locked the second door. This time his hands weren't trembling. Despite Klaus's frantic barking, Alex felt more in control. Klaus might be smart, but there was no way he could figure out what Alex was about to do—use himself for bait. The whole plan depended on speed, and luckily, speed with a fast takeoff and quick delivery was his specialty. He took long, deep breaths, in and out, in and out, filling his lungs the way he did before a race.

He was ready. He stood by the second cage door and shook it to get Klaus's attention. He even tried to whistle, but nothing came out except a pathetic burst of air. It didn't matter. Klaus was already wild to get in, scratching and pawing at the fencing so hard his nails made the wires sing. Alex stuck his fingers through the wiring and unlocked the cage door, grateful the doors opened outward, not inward. Slowly he pushed the door ajar about two inches, just enough, he hoped, to entice Klaus to claw at it until he opened it the whole way.

The trick worked. Alex had counted on Klaus being intelligent enough to realize he could open the door, and he was. The dog worked at the door with his nose, dug at it with his paws, even shouldered it until it was open far enough for him to get his head through. It would be only moments before he was in the cage with Alex. Time to get out of here!

Alex raced to the little connecting gate between the two cages, dropped to his hands and knees and scrambled through, letting it swing shut behind him. As he tried to stand up, he stumbled and almost fell. It was like some lousy obstacle course, only with Klaus barking furiously behind him, Alex knew more was at stake than passing a gym test. He glanced over his shoulder. "Never look back at your competition" was the cardinal rule of track. But Alex couldn't resist. Klaus was already in the far cage and headed for the little connecting gate. He barreled through it just as Alex unlocked the door to the first cage, slipped through, and slammed it shut behind him. Alex felt the full weight of Klaus's body bend the wires as the dog leaped against the door with his fangs bared. Quickly Alex latched the hook as Klaus backed up and attacked the wires again in a barking fury of frustration. Now Klaus was on the inside and Alex on the outside. But Alex wasn't safe yet. That second cage door was still wide open where Klaus had nosed it ajar.

Now was Alex's moment for real speed. He took off, accelerating in split seconds as he ran around the outside of both cages to reach the open door on the second cage before the dog did. Alex had to shut and lock it before the dog realized it was his only way out of either cage. There was no underestimating Klaus. He had already run through the connecting gate between the two cages by the time Alex reached the open door and shoved it shut. This time there was no mistaking how badly his hands trembled. He could hardly grasp the little hook. There, it was locked. He'd done it. Both cage doors were locked with Klaus inside.

Safe, Alex was safe. Klaus knew it too. He barked and barked, but no longer threw himself against the wires. Instead he just paced back and forth, snarling and growling like a caged animal in a zoo.

Right now what Alex needed was to get away from the sight of that dog. Klaus had been out to kill him and had almost succeeded. For the first time, Alex knew what the words "attack dog" meant. As he stumbled away from the cages back along the side of the barn, hot bile filled his throat. He tried to swallow it back down, but couldn't. He threw up violently, over and over. It left him so weak, he sank to the ground and just lay on the damp grass taking deep breaths. He'd never thrown up at a track meet like a lot of the guys did, but now he knew how they felt.

Alex rolled over on his back and looked up at the sky.

It was a nothing kind of sky, not blue or gray, just Pennsylvania clouds and haze hanging there, heavy with heat. Alex watched a long, low cloud slowly regroup and change shape. Other clouds drifted around it, forming a slow-motion background. He didn't think, he just watched. He was wiped clean, incapable of thinking. He only vaguely wondered what the wheezing sound was he heard. It was his breath, that's what it was, rattling in his throat. And his mouth was filled with the bitter taste of vomit.

Alex might not have wanted to think, but the process resumed without his conscious choice. Something was wrong here at Red Roof Farm, terribly wrong. There was no getting around it. The dog's unprovoked attack, the cars that didn't work, the plants that were freshly watered. None of it made sense. All he knew was that he was being sucked into something out of his control and beyond his understanding. And he wanted no part of it.

Alex got up from the grass and blew his nose. He'd take a swim in the pool to wash off, pick up his duffel bag from the cottage and leave. If the jeep didn't work, he'd phone for a cab. If the phone didn't work, he'd walk every step of the way, and this time nothing could stop him.

Nine...

Still dazed from his encounter with Klaus, Alex was in the pool naked when the blue Ford barreled around the corner of the house, taking the curve much too fast. Its front wheels careened off the hardtop and skidded. The tires burrowed deep tracks in the soft earth as it came to a screeching stop.

Klaus reacted by barking harder than ever. But Alex couldn't have uttered a sound if he had wanted to. Openmouthed, he stood paralyzed in the shallow end of the pool, staring. The car was a new two-door Pinto. That much he registered on. But it might as well have been a spaceship from another planet for all Alex could comprehend what its appearance could possibly mean.

The driver's door opened and a figure stepped out. Alex didn't have his glasses on, but he could see the person was tall and wore a huge sombrero, red shirt and cowboy boots. It was a costume the way all those outfits in the Baron's bedroom closet were costumes. Naked, trapped, vulnerable, Alex stared as the figure looked at the house, studying it. Then the stranger turned toward the barn as if trying to figure out what the barking was all about. His glance swung toward the pool. And Alex. He saw Alex.

With long, loose strides, he headed down the driveway, the rowels on his spurs jangling and his face a dark shadow under the wide sombrero. Alex didn't try to duck underwater or swim or run or yell or anything. He just stood frozen, beyond terror.

Incredibly, the stranger laughed as he leaned down by the edge of the pool and stuck out his hand. "You look like you're in an advanced state of apoplexy. I'm not that much of a surprise, am I?" he demanded.

Alex stared at the outstretched hand without making a move to take it. He couldn't. Not one muscle in his whole body worked, and he was as cold as if he had been standing in the Arctic Ocean instead of a lukewarm pool in Pennsylvania.

The stranger laughed again, but not so convincingly this time. He lowered his hand. "Hey, what's with you, kid?"

Somewhere deep inside him, Alex knew that the voice and the laugh were familiar. So was the face. But before he could get it together, the other person stood up and walked around to the pool steps so that only a few feet of water separated the two of them. "It's me, Bruce Rogers Buchanan, here in the flesh to enjoy the summer of a lifetime."

Bruce Buchanan! Of course it was Bruce. "I . . . I . . . thought you were in Mexico."

"Mexico was getting to be a drag. I planned to stay another week but the girl I was with had to meet her parents so I vamoosed, as the expression goes."

At least Alex reacted to that. Bruce had taken his own

sweet time getting here and could have cared less about Alex *or* the job. One good thing, Alex's anger got his juices going again. He waded over to the steps and climbed up them, suddenly aware of how thin he was, with his bony rib cage and long skinny feet. Bruce was tanned almost black and his new brush mustache made him seem more like twenty-five than nineteen. His dark brows met in a straight line over his eyes, and with his Mexican outfit he looked like a handsome Mexican bandit straight out of a grade B movie. Alex grabbed for his glasses and put them on. For some dumb reason, he felt even more naked without his glasses than without his clothes.

"Welcome to Cozy Acres," he tried to joke as he pulled on his cut-offs.

"So where were you? I phoned from Albany last night and then from Philadelphia this morning and never got an answer."

"Well . . . ah . . . I wasn't in last night and I've been working on the yard all morning." Alex tried to sound casual.

But he didn't fool Bruce. Bruce laughed. "A little spooked out by the old homestead, huh? I can't say I blame you. It's a monster."

Alex was embarrassed that Bruce had seen through him so quickly. After all, he didn't know Bruce that well. He tried to pass it off. "It's not so bad, just sorta creepy at night."

"Well, don't worry. You and me will liven it up, but good."

All of a sudden, Alex felt better. Bruce oozed confidence out of every pore the way Alex oozed sweat.

There was no way Bruce was going to imagine dead white cats killing mice, or see pale faces at windows or find keys materializing out of nowhere. That skirmish with Klaus must have sent Alex right to the edge. But Bruce was here now and everything was going to be fine. The two of them could get on with their summer just the way they'd planned. One thing for sure, Bruce was never going to hear about these past couple of days, not from Alex anyway.

Ten...

Bruce jerked his head in the direction of the barn. He and Alex were unloading the car. "What's with that dog?"

"It's the Baron's German shepherd. Don't let him out whatever you do. I mean, he went right for my throat." Alex's voice was almost a squeak. He couldn't fake being casual about that.

Bruce nodded as he handed Alex a couple of duffel bags and a tennis racket from the car trunk. "I saw those "Beware of the Dog" signs on the way in, but I thought they were a joke."

"No joke." For sure.

"Did the old man leave any liquor or beer around?"

Alex hadn't thought to check. "I don't know."

"If there isn't any, we can pick up some when I return this bomb of a Hertz." Bruce led the way up the back stairs carrying the rest of his luggage.

He dumped everything on the kitchen floor, tossed his sombrero on top, opened the refrigerator door and checked over the contents. He pulled out a plum and began to eat it as he headed through the pantry into the dining room. Alex followed, curious to see Bruce's reaction to the dining room table all set up with silver and china. But Bruce didn't say anything. He barely glanced at the table as he went straight into the living room. Alex paused at the dining room door. Bruce's total disinterest in the fancy table setting cleared Alex's head. It was no big deal after all.

By the time Alex reached the living room, Bruce was already tapping on the mahogany wall panels as if he expected them to swing open and reveal hidden rooms. Well, why not? This was certainly a hidden-room kind of house. Bruce even lifted up a couple of portraits and checked behind them, for what, Alex didn't know. Maybe a safe. Bruce was going through the house like a private eye, and Alex liked his thoroughness. Bruce knew what he was doing, all right.

"This place smells rotten," Bruce commented as he opened the patio door and left it ajar. Alex wasn't aware that the house still smelled. Maybe that meant he had gotten used to it, which was a repulsive thought. Then he noticed that Bruce was checking over the patio flagstones and right away he knew why.

"We hosed down the bloodstains," Alex said. There was no need to mention that Dad had done the whole job.

Bruce came back into the living room. "The old man killed himself after shooting his wife and the cat, huh?"

Bruce didn't have to go into all this. Dad had sent him the newspaper clipping and he knew perfectly well what had happened.

"Yeah, I guess so," Alex mumbled.

All of a sudden, Bruce whipped his hand out of his pocket as if he were pulling out a gun. With his forefinger pointed straight out like a gun barrel, he crouched low and tiptoed into the den. As he circled around the desk into the center of the room, he put his finger to his lips for silence.

"Shh," he whispered. "She's sitting at the desk. Maybe she noticed me sneak into the room and maybe not. She might even have looked up and smiled. Then she turned back to whatever she was doing, typing, see, and I move in closer. And closer. I raise my gun slowly to her head. POW! I drill her."

Alex's stomach lurched just like it had before, and the same hot taste of bile filled his mouth. But this time he kept everything down. Bruce didn't have to make it so graphic. He was forcing Alex to picture the whole scene—the explosion, the burst of blood, the small crumpled body falling off the chair. Somehow knowing what the Baroness looked like made it even worse. Alex ran his hand across his dry lips.

Bruce grinned as if he knew what Alex were thinking. Then he walked over to the window, pulled back the draperies and looked out before letting them fall back in place. "I guess I'll take my stuff upstairs and get unpacked," he announced.

Alex wasn't listening. He still felt shaken. But that was ridiculous. If he were going to spend all summer in this house, he had better accept the facts of what happened like Bruce had. He forced himself to look at the paneling over the desk where the bullet had shattered the wood into jagged red splinters. From there his eyes traveled down to the stain on the rug, then up again to the typewriter on the desk. For the first time he wondered what the Baroness had been doing when she was killed. Probably typing, like Bruce said. But there was no paper in the typewriter, and the police hadn't taken anything. At least Dad had said the police had found no note of any kind.

Still, she must have been working on something. Alex opened the middle desk drawer to see if there was anything of interest in it, but all he found were stamps and stationery and paper clips and pencils. The other drawers were neatly arranged with the usual desk paraphernalia too, more stationery, cancelled checks, bankbooks, address books and two drawers filled with manila envelopes labeled, *Medical, Insurance, Taxes, Social Security, Stocks*. Nothing was out of order.

Now Alex's curiosity was really aroused. He began to tap on the wall panels like Bruce had, just in case one might conceal a hollow hiding place. As he moved around the desk, he knocked over the wastebasket with his foot. When he righted it, he noticed a piece of paper inside. Only it wasn't a piece of paper, it was an envelope. He pulled it out and read the typewritten address.

> Mr. George A. Phillips
> Walcott, McHugh, Bower & Phillips
> 22 Hemphill Street
> Boston, Massachusetts 02103

It was Dad's name on the envelope. It was not only Dad's name, but Dad's law firm address as well.

Eleven...

"Hey, Alex, come here and take a look at this."

It was Bruce yelling from upstairs. Alex didn't reply. He chewed his lip as he studied Dad's address on the envelope. The Baroness must have been typing a letter to Dad when the Baron shot her, and it must have been a business letter because the envelope was addressed to his office. So where was the letter? Dad had said the police had found no note or letter of any kind, which eliminated the police having it. Maybe the Baron had taken it after he had killed her. That was a possibility. Another possibility was the Baroness had hidden the letter somewhere. On the other hand, she may have been shot before she ever wrote the letter. All of which left everything right where it was before, in a big question mark.

"Alex, c'mon up here." Bruce's voice was impatient.

Alex would have to think more about this later. He slid the envelope in the middle drawer and headed upstairs. Bruce was waiting for him at the far end of the hall in the master-bedroom doorway. His grin was so broad his teeth practically glowed white in his dark face.

Alex had been in the master bedroom before, the day he had arrived. A king-sized canopied bed in the center of the room had red curtains looped back to four posters. Matching red draperies hung at the windows. Prints and etchings and old engravings covered the flocked red wallpaper.

Bruce led the way over to a big closet. Alex already knew what was inside, all those costumes. Sure enough, Bruce disappeared and came out wearing a cape and a top hat set on his head at a rakish angle. He did a quick little dance step into the bedroom, then tapped his way back into the closet. Alex had to laugh. Bruce was great. While Alex went around concocting gory fantasies, Bruce saw the funny side of everything. Still laughing, Alex followed Bruce into the walk-in closet.

Bright fluorescent lights spurted overhead, throwing a harsh glare on the racks of clothes—jackets, slacks, coats, dressing gowns, skirts, dresses, robes—all in shades of red. Alex recognized some of the costumes from the pictures in the photograph albums.

"Man, these dudes must have been crazy." Bruce's voice from the back of the closet was muffled. He was bent over a stack of hat boxes. When he straightened up, he had exchanged the top hat for a red velvet turban that was so small it barely fit the top of his head. In place of the cape he held up a strapless red evening dress that only came to his knees. With his blue jeans and cowboy boots sticking out from under the skirt, he looked ridiculous.

"Oh, Bruce, you're adorrrable," Alex mocked.

It was all the encouragement Bruce needed. He started to prance around the room with the dress, kicking up his heels and singing in a screeching falsetto. Now Alex was really laughing, and the sillier Bruce got, the harder he laughed. He tried to stop, but couldn't. And then it hit him. He'd better get to a bathroom, and fast.

There was a door just off the bedroom. It was the Baron's dressing room with a bathroom beyond. Alex made it just in time. When he came out, he was completely sober. Wow, it had been some day. He sank down on one of the dressing room chairs to catch his breath. He was beat. As Alex looked around, he realized the dressing room was decorated just like the bedroom, with a red rug, red curtains, and red wallpaper. But something fluttering out the dressing room closet door wasn't red. It was yellow.

The sight of anything yellow was so out of place in all this suffocating red, Alex got up to check it out. It was a woman's scarf caught in the closet door. Alex pulled on it, but it wouldn't budge. And the closet was locked. Alex took his Swiss Army knife from his pocket, opened one of the blades, and tried to unlock the door. But it didn't work.

"What are you doing?" Bruce stood in the doorway.

"I want to get in this closet."

"No problem."

Bruce pulled a credit card from his wallet and kneeled by the door. He still had on his absurd velvet turban, but he was all seriousness as he slid the stiff card between the door and the lock and turned the knob at the same time. The closet door opened.

Trust Bruce to take care of it. Alex reached for the yellow scarf. It was knotted over the inside knob as if it had been put there deliberately. Alex untied it and, without thinking, draped it around his neck. Immediately, he noticed the strong cigarette smell that clung to it. The combination of the cigarette odor and its bright yellow color meant it must have belonged to the Baroness. Without saying anything to Bruce, Alex followed him inside the closet.

It was a walk-in closet like the one in the master bedroom, but this one was set up as an office with bookshelves, a filing cabinet, racks of slides and movie reels, a film projector and a built-in desk. Bruce headed right for a Leica camera and held it up to his eye, snapping imaginary pictures.

"What a great camera, and it's got a whole roll of unused film on it. We can take pictures all summer." Bruce put the camera down and moved over to the bookshelves. He pulled a book out and flipped through it. Looking over his shoulder, Alex saw it was some kind of military book written in German.

"Here, let me see." Alex took it from Bruce and opened to the first page, a formal picture of Adolph Hitler. The photographs in the rest of the book were of soldiers, some stiffly posed and some taken on the battlefield. Alex didn't have to be a genius to know they all wore German Army uniforms. He'd seen his share of World War II movies on TV.

"So the old Baron was a Nazi, huh? It figures," Bruce commented. He must have seen the same movies.

Alex put the book back and pulled out another. It was a German military text full of diagrams and maps and charts. Disappointed, Alex ran his finger along the row of books, hoping to find one in English. His finger paused, backed up, and stopped at a set of photograph albums. They were the war year albums that were missing from the downstairs library. Alex took out the first one, 1937–1939.

The Baron with his big ears and thin face was unmistakable. He wore a German Army uniform in every picture. Alex wasn't surprised. He already knew that the Baron was a big Nazi-type. Alex replaced the album and took out another, 1942–1944. There were more pictures of the Baron, still in uniform, but with lots of medals and ribbons now. He seemed older and more serious than the few years between the albums would merit.

For the first time there were pictures of the Baroness, too, sometimes with the Baron, sometimes with an older couple and two young soldiers who must have been her family, and frequently with Nazi officers. In one picture she had an army cap tilted back on her head with her arms around the shoulders of two officers.

Bruce was busy rummaging in a foot locker and hadn't noticed Alex going through the albums. Slowly Alex put them back. Nazis, both of them. He expected as much from the Baron, but he felt differently about the Baroness. Her messy, sunny cottage had appealed to him and he'd really liked her paintings. He somehow felt she had let him down.

"Get a load of this."

Bruce had strewn the contents of the foot locker all over, big red flags emblazoned with swastikas, German uniforms reeking of mothballs, ribbons, medals, citations, a helmet, a sword. His mind still on the Baroness, Alex stared dully at the display. Then a label on one of the boxes caught his eye—"American Socialist Rights Party." It nudged a memory. Alex opened the box. Inside were papers and brochures with swastikas on the letterheads. Alex glanced through one of the brochures. Though it was in English, it was all Nazi propaganda.

Wait a minute. No wonder that name was familiar. Wasn't that the organization that had inherited the Von Dursts' house, property and all their belongings? Alex was sure he remembered his father telling him that and saying he planned to check out who they were because he had never heard of them. Not only that, but Dad had said that for tax purposes, Red Roof Farm had been in the Baroness's name. That meant she had willed everything to some Nazi organization. But that was terrible! How could she? Any sympathy Alex might have felt for her earlier was completely gone.

Alex knew all about the Nazis. He had studied the Holocaust in school this year. Six million Jews exterminated. Even when Alex had read those figures in his textbook, he'd found it hard to believe.

Bruce had already put on the pants to one of the Nazi uniforms and was slipping into the jacket. It was a perfect fit. Alex hardly noticed. He was in shock. If only that scarf hadn't led him into this closet he'd never even have known the Baroness was a total Nazi. All of a sudden, he sucked in his breath. Slowly he turned to face the window. It was shut and the draperies were drawn. And yet that scarf had been fluttering back and forth. Was he losing his mind? There was not one breath of air stirring in the room.

He was sure the yellow scarf belonged to the Baroness. It was almost as though her scarf had been leading him on, as if he were supposed to find all this Nazi stuff in the closet. Alex looked over at Bruce who was putting an officer's cap on in front of the mirror. Bruce obviously hadn't noticed anything. Maybe Alex *was* crazy. Or maybe these weird red rooms were finally getting to him. Either way, Alex wanted out of here. He yanked the scarf from around his neck as if it were choking him and rushed from the room.

...Twelve

"This is my friend who's staying at Red Roof Farm with me, Bruce Buchanan. This is Joanna . . . uh . . . and Sherrie . . . uh . . ." Alex made his usual smooth introductions as he forgot both girls' last names. It was three days since Bruce had arrived, but what with taking the Hertz car back and getting settled, it was the first chance they'd had to drive to town.

"Hi, Sherrie Uh and Joanna Uh. Wye Mills is beginning to look up." Bruce grinned his white-teeth-in-a-tan-face grin.

"Hi, Bruce. Nice to meet you." Sherrie smiled and two dimples punctuated her cheeks. Alex had never noticed she had dimples before, but maybe that was because he had never seen her smile before.

Bruce pushed his sombrero back on his head and leaned against the counter opposite Sherrie. "Alex says you two live around here. Seeing as how we're gonna be at Red Roof Farm all summer, I reckon we're gonna git purty lonesome. Mebbe you gals can show us the local action."

From what he'd seen of Sherrie, Alex guessed she

knew the local action pretty well. But she shrugged her shoulders. "There's absolutely no action at all, believe me."

"There will be now that Alex and me have hit town—right, pardner?" Bruce nudged Alex.

"Oh yeah, right. You'd better believe it." Alex's heartiness sounded forced. He wished he could pull off that mock macho routine like Bruce.

Bruce turned to Joanna who still hadn't said anything. "Alex and I decided it would be great if you girls came out to the farm tomorrow for a cookout. We'll even let you do the cooking."

Joanna grinned at Bruce as if to tell him he wasn't fooling her for a minute, but when she answered she looked at Alex. "You wouldn't be able to eat it. I'm a terrible cook."

Alex grinned back. "I'll do the cooking," he said, "but only if you promise to come for a swim too."

Sherrie arranged her face in a pout. "Joanna and me are going to the Jersey shore for two weeks with Mom and Dad. We're closing the store. Didn't you see the sign out front?"

What? That was rotten. "Two weeks?" Alex's voice cracked. It hadn't done that in a long time.

"I've never seen the ocean and I can't wait." Joanna's whole face radiated excitement.

Alex knew how she felt. He had never flown in a plane until last year, and he still remembered the thrill of it. Nevertheless, the girls being gone didn't help Bruce and him any.

Joanna and Sherrie walked them out to the pickup.

They seemed to pair off naturally, Sherrie with Bruce, and Joanna with Alex, and that was fine with Alex. More than fine, perfect.

"Am I glad you showed up with Bruce," Joanna said in a low voice. "Sherrie broke up with her boyfriend last week and she's driving me crazy moaning and groaning about it. I can tell she likes Bruce. Maybe she'll be easier to live with if she knows he's going to be around when we get back."

Alex nodded, trying not to show his disappointment. Two weeks sounded like forever. He climbed into the passenger side and shut the door. "So long, Joanna. Have a good time."

Unexpectedly, Joanna stuck her head in the open window. "I'm even gladder you showed up, Alex. I think we're going to get along fine too." She blushed as she said it. Alex wondered if he were blushing. He certainly felt hot.

With the girls gone, the days dragged. First of all, it hardly stopped raining so that Alex and Bruce had to cut the lawn and do the yard work between showers. And it was hot, a heavy, leaden, drag-you-down kind of hot. When it wasn't raining, it was steaming. All the furniture in the house was sticky, as if layers of wax were melting in the humidity. Even swimming in the pool didn't help. For excitement Alex tried to grow a mustache, but it only came out a blond fuzz.

And Alex was bothered by a lot of headaches. They were due partly to the weather, but mostly to Bruce. A couple of days after Bruce arrived, he had discovered the Baron's gun collection in the basement with enough ammunition for an army. Bruce was in ecstasy. He and his father were big hunters. Right away he set up a shooting target outside and practiced every spare moment. Alex got so tired of the constant sound of gunfire, he finally resorted to stuffing cotton in his ears.

The one thing that made him feel better was Klaus. The morning after he and Bruce had found the Baron's Nazi closet, Alex had passed Klaus's cage on his way to the compost pile. Instead of leaping into his usual frenzied rage, Klaus barked and wagged his tail. Alex approached the cage cautiously. Klaus ran right over and nuzzled his nose against the wires, his tail swinging back and forth like a metronome. Carefully, very carefully, Alex wiggled his fingers through the cage, ready to snatch them out at the first sign of hostility. But Klaus touched his nose against them in friendship.

As the days went on, the bond between them grew. Alex took over Klaus's care and feeding from Bruce. He even entered Klaus's cage and brushed his tangled coat. But it wasn't until the day they roughhoused that Alex knew he could trust Klaus completely. After that, the cage was forgotten. Klaus followed Alex everywhere, padded after him as he worked, went swimming with him, and even slept at the foot of his bed.

Not only had things changed with Klaus, but Alex felt more relaxed about living at Red Roof Farm too. Maybe it was Bruce's matter-of-fact way of looking at things. Or maybe it was because there were no more bizarre incidents like he'd experienced when he first arrived. It was only now, with the perspective of time, that Alex was able to admit that he'd almost believed some mysterious extradimensional forces had been hassling him. Those first few days alone must have made him a little flaky. At least he had never confided in Bruce. Bruce would have laughed his head off.

Now, with all that behind him, he and Bruce settled into a kind of routine. They went into town a couple of nights, but Sherrie had been right about Wye Mills. It was dead. Mostly they watched TV. Then one night, Bruce remembered the Nazi films in the Baron's closet. He got out the projector and screen and set everything up. He didn't bother with the sound track, figuring it was in German anyway. But seeing Hitler pound his fists and rant and rave in complete silence was eerie. And all the time Alex was watching, he was thinking about the films of the concentration camp survivors he'd seen in social studies class when they'd studied the Holocaust—gaunt, hollow-eyed skeletons in striped pajamas clinging to barbed-wire fencing. He was so enraged at the thought of the Von Dursts sitting around in their stupid red costumes enjoying these films, he didn't even hear the phone ring until Bruce got up to answer it.

Bruce wasn't gone long. "The girls are back. They got sick of the rain at the shore and came home two days early."

Alex hadn't even noticed it was raining again. It was so constant, he must have gotten used to its patter on the tile roof and the gurgle of water running down the drain pipes. Then he registered on what Bruce had said. The girls were back. That was the best news he had heard in weeks. But for some reason, he could hardly remember what Joanna looked like. That was all right. He remembered that he liked her. He rubbed his fingers over his mustache. It hadn't grown much beyond the down stage yet. He'd get a good look at it in the morning and decide then whether or not to shave it off.

"They're coming out tomorrow about five for a swim. A swimmmm, baby." Bruce drawled out the words with an exaggerated leer. He had lost most of his Mexican tan, but his teeth still looked Gleem-white under his black mustache.

Unbelievably, the next day turned out to be clear, hot but clear. Alex and Bruce opened all the windows and got to work cleaning. They hadn't done anything inside since they'd arrived and the place was a disaster. The house was stocked with so much china and crystal, they had just kept using new plates and glasses without bothering to wash the old. And for the first time Alex was aware of little gnats hovering over the sink and a distinct smell of rotten food. Used frozen TV-dinner trays, pizza boxes and a million empty beer cans compounded the mess. Alex stuffed all the trash into garbage bags and carried them outside. But the garbage cans were full. What they needed was a trash pickup. Alex checked the phone list on the kitchen bulletin board. There it was, Malone's Disposal Company. Alex phoned the number and left a message with the answering service for a pickup at Red Roof Farm.

As Alex loaded the dishwasher, he heard the vacuum cleaner start up in the next room. The shrill whine must have frightened Klaus. The dog barreled past Alex, out the open back door and off into the woods. As he laughed over Klaus's ridiculous reaction to the vacuum cleaner, Alex finished up the dishes, then filled the watering can to take care of the plants. He had been watering them all along, but they looked practically dead. He had probably watered them too much. Well, he had never promised to keep a bunch of plants going. And he'd totally forgotten the ones in the cottage. He'd toss them out next time he was down there.

Bruce appeared in the doorway holding a dust rag and a can of furniture polish. Alex had to hand it to Bruce. He could get away with almost anything and not look foolish.

"Put a couple of six-packs in the refrigerator, will you?" Bruce called in.

Alex went downstairs to the basement cooler, took out the beer and raced back up. The Baron had arranged the basement as an indoor target range, and the bullet-riddled paper-deer and paper-men targets really turned Alex off.

He opened the refrigerator door and pushed everything over on the bottom shelf to make room for the beer. His hand froze in position. The insulin bottle was way in the back right where he'd put it weeks ago. But it was three-quarters empty. Alex pulled the bottle out. He distinctly remembered it had been almost full when he first saw it. He checked the top. He turned it upside down to see if anything leaked out. The bottle was airtight.

What was going on? *He* certainly hadn't been taking the insulin, and he knew Bruce hadn't either. Then who had? Only one name came to mind. The Baroness. But that was idiotic. The Baroness was totally, certifiably, autopsied dead.

Without meaning to, Alex glanced over at the lifeless plants by the window. He had killed them off, for certain. But someone—or something—had watered them and kept them alive during the weeks before he'd arrived. And those plants in Libertas Cottage had been watered and cared for too. He had pushed those thoughts deliberately out of his mind for a long time. Now he had to face them. There was no way plants in an empty house could stay freshly watered, or insulin in an airtight bottle could gradually disappear, or for that matter, a yellow scarf ripple back and forth in an airtight room . . . unless . . . unless . . . there was some power beyond his comprehension at work here at Red Roof Farm.

No! Alex didn't know whether he shouted the word out loud or not. It didn't matter. He had to stop thinking that way. He was letting his imagination panic his good sense, and he refused, absolutely refused, to go that route again.

It was easy enough to tell himself that, but the old familiar band of iron squeezed his chest so tight he could hardly breathe. And the insulin bottle felt as cold as ice in his hand.

...Thirteen

Joanna and Sherrie were due at five, but didn't show up until almost six. Sherrie was driving a beat-up old VW with a purple paint job corroded with rust. Joanna got out first.

"Hi, Alex."

Alex had forgotten how tall Joanna was, even taller than he. He checked her feet and was relieved to see she was wearing high-heeled clogs. Then Sherrie got out. She had on a spectacular halter-and-shorts outfit that would be easy to get excited about. And Bruce looked excited.

"Woof, woof. Welcome to Wed Woof Farm, my fair beauties." He bowed and stroked his mustache like an old-time villain.

Both girls laughed and Alex had to laugh too. Bruce got away with murder. He usually said exactly what he was thinking, but he always made it sound as if he were kidding.

"What a creepy looking place, huh, Joanna?" Sherrie pulled a pack of cigarettes from her pocket and lit one. The two girls stared at the house and Alex remembered staring the same way when he'd first seen it.

"I can't wait to see inside, especially where all the

murders were. How about a tour, Bruce?" Sherrie started up the back steps without waiting for an answer, her backless sandals flopping.

Bruce ran up the stairs after her. "You'll freak out when you see the bedroom." He put his arm around Sherrie's shoulders and the two of them went inside, leaving Alex and Joanna standing by the car.

"Do you want to go in too?" Alex hoped Joanna would say no. He'd had his fill of the Von Dursts for one afternoon and he was determined to put the whole insulin business out of his mind.

His voice must have conveyed how he felt. "Maybe later," Joanna answered. "Sherrie told me about that man killing his wife and his cat and himself and I think the whole thing is sick. What I'd really like to do is to hit the pool. Uncle Paul's store isn't air-conditioned, and I'm so hot I'm about to expire. We hardly swam at the shore at all. If it wasn't raining, the surf was too rough to go in."

Alex had never heard Joanna put more than ten words together before. He had a hunch Joanna didn't say much of anything when Sherrie was around. He felt the same way.

As if in consensus, the two of them started walking toward the pool. "What's the difference in age between you and Sherrie anyway?" Alex made a point of not asking Joanna her age in case she was older than he.

"More than two years. Sherrie is nineteen and I won't be seventeen until October."

"October what?" Alex leaned over and picked a blade of grass to suck on.

"Sixth."

"You're kidding. My birthday's October seventh and

I'll be seventeen too. That's incredible. Our chances of being almost twins is like two out of three-sixty-five." It was amazing. Exactly the same age. Joanna wasn't older after all. Alex reached down and took her hand.

Joanna pushed the damp tendrils of blonde hair back from her face. "How do you and Bruce get along? Sherrie and I are so different we fight and bicker all the time."

"Bruce is nearly twenty and in college so he really knows what's going on. He's a great guy and always kidding around, you know, and fun to be with." But as soon as the words were out, Alex realized that wasn't completely true. When he and Bruce were alone, Bruce didn't kid around at all. In fact, he hardly even talked to Alex. And for sure, he never did his share of the work. Most of the time he practiced his shooting or just lay around drinking beer and watching TV. "Bruce has got a thing about guns. The Baron had a big gun collection and Bruce target shoots every day."

"Ugh, I hate guns."

Alex looked at Joanna with new interest. They agreed on practically everything. And he couldn't get over the coincidence of their birthdays. Still, Alex felt he had to defend Bruce. "Everyone in upstate New York hunts. I know Bruce and his father go out for their bucks every fall."

They had reached the pool. Joanna spread her beach towel on the ground, unzipped her cut-offs and stepped out of them. Then she pulled off her blouse and slipped out of her clogs. She was wearing a green bikini and Alex couldn't help noticing her ribs stuck out like his. Not that she was all that thin, but she certainly wasn't built like Sherrie. Alex had on his bathing suit under his clothes too. He took off his shorts and sat down on the towel next to Joanna.

"I didn't even get a tan at the shore," Joanna complained as she lay down on her back and closed her eyes. "I'm white as a ghost."

Wrong word, Alex thought, as his mind immediately and without his volition, turned to the Baroness. He stared off into the woods. When Alex had asked, Bruce had sworn he had never even noticed the insulin, let alone spilled any. The ramifications of what might have happened to the insulin alarmed Alex in a strange way, not physically, but intellectually or cerebrally, or whatever mental fear was called. Alex looked at Joanna, the flag-blue sky, the rolling green hills beyond the woods. All those were reality. The insulin, the plants, the fluttering scarf were unreality. Impossibilities. And yet . . . and yet . . .

Neither Alex nor Joanna spoke for a long time. Then Joanna sighed.

"Sometimes I think Sherrie and I will kill each other before I leave the end of August."

"How come you're visiting for so long?" It was an effort for Alex to pull himself back.

"My parents went to Europe and they don't trust me to stay alone in Milwaukee, if you can believe it."

Another tie between them. "I believe it, all right. My parents are exactly the same. I was amazed they let me take this job."

"All Sherrie talks about is her old boyfriend, George Duffy, and how much she hates him." Joanna squinted her eyes against the sun that was low in the western sky and smiled her nice warm smile. "For a while I figured the summer was a totally lost cause, but I think I've changed my mind."

Alex smiled back. "You know, I don't have to stay here at the Farm every second. We could go to Philadelphia some day, just the two of us without Bruce or Sherrie."

"Hey, why not?" Joanna sat right up. "I'm off on Thursdays and—"

"Joanna! Alex! Listen, have I got an idea!"

Joanna and Alex turned around. Sherrie was running across the backyard toward them. She was wearing one of the Baroness's dresses, a red satin evening gown that fit perfectly. Tiny red feathers blew off the hem as she ran. Bruce, engrossed in examining a camera, followed behind.

"We're going to throw a costume party. Isn't that a brainstorm?" Sherrie sang out.

Alex had no idea what she was talking about. Neither, apparently, did Joanna. "A what?" she asked.

"Jo, you wouldn't believe those closets. They are full of the weirdest costumes you ever saw, like this thing I have on. They're all in red and there are hundreds of them. We can round up all the kids who are home and throw a big costume party."

Sherrie was talking so fast Alex didn't catch everything, but he got the gist of it. "I don't know, Sherrie. What do you think, Bruce?"

"I think we'll stagnate out here if we don't do something. We can charge everyone an entrance fee, hire a band, and Sherrie says her father can get us beer and food wholesale. Kids will be crazy to get in here and check out the big murder scene."

Probably those costumes would all end up as rummage anyway, but somehow the whole idea rubbed Alex the wrong way. "Maybe we ought to think it over."

Joanna frowned. "It's a terrible idea. Everybody within a hundred miles would come. They'd wreck the house and everything in it."

"Joanna Hebbel, you are so straight I can't believe it. You think Bruce and Alex can't control a party?" Sherrie's pout wasn't a put-on. She was really angry.

"Since it's none of my business anyway, I'm going for a swim." Joanna walked over to the diving board and Alex could tell by the square set of her shoulders that she was as angry as Sherrie. Even Bruce looked annoyed as he led Sherrie over to the pool to take her picture.

Alex decided to leave until everyone cooled down. He'd go in the house for a Coke. He put his sneakers back on, wiped off his steamy glasses with his towel and started up the driveway. His untied sneaker laces clicked on the hardtop.

"Rorrff."

The familiar bark immediately picked up Alex's spirits. It must be Klaus coming back from his excursion in the woods. He'd been gone since morning. Klaus loved the woods and always came back exhausted and covered with brambles and leaves. Alex looked across the yard. His glasses were smeared where he had tried to dry them, but even so he could see Klaus tear out of the woods, his powerful legs eating up the distance between them.

Alex gave a sharp whistle through his teeth.

That was strange. Usually Klaus stopped short at Alex's whistle and waited for an order. But now he just kept running full speed up the sloping backyard. He skirted around the pool, never even glancing at Joanna splashing through the water in a fury of foam and waves, or at Bruce and Sherrie busy with their picture-taking. Klaus was headed straight for Alex. All of a sudden, the single-minded thrust of the dog reminded Alex of the first time he had seen Klaus, the day Klaus had attacked him. The dog's ears were flat against his head the same way now. Saliva spun from his open mouth and his fangs were bared.

This wasn't Alex's affectionate companion running in answer to his master's whistle. This was an eighty-pound German shepherd guard dog, trained to attack. And kill.

Fourteen...

Klaus had already reached the driveway. Alex had to get out of here. But he had nowhere to go. There weren't any trees around to climb and he'd never make the back porch in time. Sherrie's VW. If he could get inside, he'd be safe.

"Alex, run!" Joanna shouted.

He didn't need any urging. He accelerated with a burst of initial speed, and this time he didn't turn around to check the competition. He didn't have to. He could hear Klaus panting right behind him, and the words "hot on his heels" had new meaning. There wasn't time to open the VW door and get inside. With a takeoff that would have done credit to his best long jump, Alex leaped onto the car hood.

But his agility was to his disadvantage. He vaulted almost completely over the car. He stopped himself just in time, but in regaining his balance, his left leg slipped off the hood almost to the ground. With a snarl of rage, Klaus sprang. His jaws snapped shut like a trap. Luckily Alex's untied sneaker was half off and, instead of getting a chunk of flesh, all Klaus got was a mouthful of sneaker. The surprise tumbled him backward. It was the second Alex needed to draw his left leg up and scramble over the windshield onto the car roof.

Alex pulled his long legs up under him and sat crosslegged, cursing the size of the tiny roof. Wild with frustration, Klaus leaped at the car. Alex could feel the force of the dog's fury shake the flimsy VW. And with each attack, Klaus was jumping higher and closer.

"Stand up, Alex!" That was Joanna again.

Standing was no good. The VW was wobbling too much for Alex to keep his balance. He'd have to kneel. That would not only concentrate his weight in the center of the roof, but also keep him at the farthest distance from the dog. But the hot metal seared his knees. He sucked in his breath with the shock of it, but didn't dare move.

Klaus immediately reacted to the new situation. He stopped his frantic assault on the car and began to pace back and forth as if he were working out a new plan of attack. Alex had never underestimated the dog's intelligence, and he didn't now. His heart was beating hard enough to burst through his rib cage.

Klaus, his friend. It wasn't the same dog. This was a disciplined dog, trained to attack and obedient to his master. Alex wasn't kidding himself any longer that he was Klaus's master. No, the dog answered to one master only, and Alex knew, dead or not, that one master was the Baron and always would be. It was the only possible explanation for why Klaus had attacked like this after their weeks of friendship. That realization frightened Alex almost as much as Klaus's powerful jaws and vicious teeth.

Abruptly Klaus stopped his pacing and started

barking sharp staccato yelps. Afraid to look down but even more afraid not to, Alex peered over the edge. Klaus had moved fifteen feet or so away from the VW. Giving himself a running start, the dog leaped as high as he could at the car and smashed against it with his whole weight. It was an amazing jump. His head showed above the roof, his black mouth open and his pink tongue glistening with saliva. Alex drew in his breath. He knew enough from track to realize that if Klaus continued, he'd leap higher and closer with each try.

"Help!" Alex shouted. "Help!"

Where was everyone? For the first time he looked toward the pool. Joanna and Sherrie clung to each other by the diving board. They were pale and their eyes were wide with fear. But Alex didn't see Bruce. There he was, sneaking across the backyard toward the house, one careful step at a time. He was going for help. It was a brave move, and Alex owed it to Bruce to keep Klaus distracted.

"Good Klaus . . . good boy . . . good dog . . ." Alex crooned low and easy the way he always talked to Klaus. But his voice wasn't up to low and easy. It was only up to weak and scared. "Good boy . . . good boy . . . good boy . . ."

Alex's meaningless chatter sent Klaus almost berserk. Now he crashed against the VW senselessly, again and again, as if he no longer cared whether he reached Alex or not. But his violence only put Alex in more danger. The VW began to rock in a rhythmic way, back and forth, back and forth. Alex slid toward one edge of the roof, then back toward the other. Now it became a matter of whether he would slide off the roof first or the car would tip over.

"Hurry, Bruce, hurry!" Alex yelled.

Thud! Thud! Eighty pounds of fury smashed against the car. It was almost over. Alex closed his eyes. He closed his mind too, refusing to think. Maybe that was why at first he wasn't even sure he heard the scream above Klaus's barking. Then he heard it again, a strange short piercing caterwaul. Alex looked over at the girls, though it hadn't come from that direction. It had seemed farther away, down by the woods.

The VW stopped rocking. Klaus dropped on all fours and stood for a moment, panting. His ears were cocked straight up and his whole body was alert. Listening.

Now there wasn't a noise to be heard but the constant background twang of summer insects. Then Klaus lifted his head and howled. Alex had never heard a wolf howl at the moon, but for some reason the comparison came to him.

Klaus turned away from the car, trotted across the driveway, past the pool, and down the sloping back-yard, picking up speed as he went. He never once looked back. His whole being was concentrated on the woods.

Alex's glasses were steamed up, but he could see something down there. It was a white flash of move-ment darting in and out behind the line of trees. It was too deep in the shadows of the woods to make out, but it was moving horizontally, as if it were trying to entice Klaus into the woods rather than escape him. Whatever it was must have been the source of that wild scream.

Now Klaus had reached the woods and the something that was leading him on disappeared. Klaus plunged into the woods and disappeared too.

"Alex, what happened? Where's the dog?" Bruce stood on the back porch, his rifle cocked.

Alex waved him away. "He's gone." It was an effort to get the words out.

The girls ran up the driveway. Still dressed in the Baroness's absurd red evening gown, Sherrie was weeping. Joanna didn't look much better. Numbly, Alex watched them approach. His body seemed to have no structure to hold it together and he knew if he tried to get off the car roof, he'd dissolve all over the ground in a formless puddle.

"It's all right . . . he's gone . . . we're safe . . ." he managed to reassure them. He was so close to being out of control, he didn't trust himself to say more. Joanna seemed to understand. She reached up, gripped his ankle and squeezed it without a word. That finished Alex. He just buried his face in his hands as wave after wave of shock shuddered over him.

...Fifteen

The girls went home right away and Big Game Hunter Bruce went off into the woods with his rifle to try and track down Klaus. Alex was glad to see everyone go. He just went into the house and sat at the kitchen table shaking for about half an hour. It must have had something to do with being in shock. He'd shaken the same way when he had totaled the family car last winter.

What Alex couldn't understand was why no one had said a word about the animal scream that had diverted Klaus and sent him running off into the woods in the first place. Bruce had been in the house and couldn't have heard it, but neither of the girls had mentioned it. It was as if no one had noticed it but he and Klaus. For sure, Klaus had. His ears had gone up like antennae and he'd taken off across the backyard like a bullet.

Alex went to the refrigerator, took out a Coke and sat back down at the table. This wasn't the first time Klaus had almost killed him. Alex remembered how docile Klaus had been that morning when he had first appeared. Then, after passively watching Alex mow the lawn for hours, he had unexpectedly made his move.

He acted as if he'd been under orders that day. And today too. There was no denying it. He and Klaus had been inseparable companions for weeks. Now this. In some unknown, unheard way, Klaus was receiving orders. But why should he attack Alex? Alex was no threat to anyone, the dead Baron included.

Alex slammed the bottle down on the table and Coke sprayed all over. He had just been through this with the Baroness and her insulin. Now he was imagining wild fantasies about the Baron giving Klaus orders. The Baron and Baroness were dead. Their bodies had been found by the police. They were buried and it had all been written up in the newspapers. Alex even had the clipping upstairs. The Baron and Baroness were over and done with.

Only . . . only . . . the Baron and Baroness weren't over and done with. Alex didn't know how or what or why, but somehow their unseen presence was a very real force at Red Roof Farm right now. Alex started shaking again as if he were cold. He *was* cold, cold with fear, physical, emotional, intellectual, every kind of fear there was. The more he thought about it, the more frantic he became. Go for a swim. Watch TV. Cook dinner. Do something, anything to stop thinking like this. But he couldn't move. He was rooted to his chair, paralyzed, vaguely aware it was getting dark out.

It was the dark that brought Bruce back. He hadn't found Klaus, but then Alex hadn't expected him to. Those woods were Klaus's second home. All Bruce turned up was a big piece of plastic polyethylene that must have been used at some time for a tarp. Bruce had picked it off a tree branch at the edge of the woods. The tarp blowing back and forth was what must have distracted Klaus from the attack, he told Alex. Alex didn't say anything. Maybe the tarp had distracted Klaus and maybe it had been something else, something bigger that moved quickly, like an animal. A white animal. A white cat. A white Persian cat.

That night Alex dreamed endless, wild dreams about Klaus, about the pool, about a costume party, about Joanna. The whole terrible day faded in and out of his consciousness all night, so when he heard a dog barking, at first it didn't waken him. Then gradually he realized it was a real dog barking. Klaus. Alex didn't open his eyes. Terrified, he lay in bed with every muscle tense.

Though the night had turned cool, Alex was soaked with sweat. Even his sheet felt damp. Then Alex was aware of something else. Slowly he opened his eyes. The barking was fading away rather than coming closer. And it had an echoey quality as if Klaus were confined in a building. Maybe he was in the barn. But that wasn't possible. Alex's room faced the front of the house and the barn was in the back.

The barking stopped. Alex waited for more, but there was none. All he could hear were the night noises of the woods and the creakings of the old house in humid weather. The moon had already set and there was no sign yet of dawn. Alex turned on the light and put on his glasses. 4:05. It didn't matter. He was going to get up. He had to see this through whether it was 4:05 or noon. And he had a pretty good idea of where he could find Klaus.

He groaned with the effort of getting out of bed. He ached all over. He hadn't realized what a physical toll that attack had taken on him. He pulled on his clothes and tiptoed from the room. The house was completely dark and a great black nothingness yawned beyond the hall bannister and down the dark staircase. Alex turned on a light. Long shadows cavorted over the walls and across the ceiling. It's your own shadow, Alex reassured himself as he made his way up the hall, but by the time he reached the master bedroom, he was almost breathless.

"Bruce, get up. We've got to find Klaus." Alex shook Bruce to waken him.

Bruce moaned, waved Alex away and turned over. Bruce always slept in the raw and his shoulders and chest were a mat of curly black hair.

He shook Bruce again. "Get your rifle. We're going out in the jeep. I know where we can find Klaus."

It must have been the word "rifle" that galvanized Bruce. He was out of bed and into his jeans without any more urging. Within ten minutes they were in the jeep and on their way up the driveway. Following Alex's directions, Bruce parked in front of Libertas Cottage. He acted surprised to see it.

"What's this place?" he asked.

"Just a guest cottage," was all Alex volunteered.

"I don't hear anything. Are you sure you know what you're doing?" Bruce complained, opening the jeep door with one hand and holding his rifle with the other.

Alex nodded, though now they were here, he wasn't so certain. At least the sky was brightening. In the few minutes it had taken them to get organized, the black night had imperceptibly advanced to gray. The morning birds were just starting up, and the crickets and katydids were at it like an army of buzz saws. Playing it safe, Alex waited in the jeep as Bruce cautiously walked up the three front steps. The porch groaned under Bruce's weight as he leaned over the railing, shone his flashlight in the front window and looked in. Right away Alex knew by the way he stiffened up that he'd seen something. He waved Alex over with his rifle.

"Klaus is in there all right, but he looks dead," Bruce said as soon as Alex had joined him.

Sure enough, when Alex looked in, he saw Klaus lying in a wide circle of blood in the middle of the room. Quickly Alex pulled out the cottage key and opened the door. Bruce pushed importantly ahead, his rifle ready.

But the rifle wasn't necessary. Though Klaus wasn't dead, he was close to it. His eyes flickered open. As soon as he saw Alex he bared his teeth, but he was too weak even to lift his head from the floor. Slowly Alex walked around him. The dog's belly had been ripped open and was still bleeding.

"Look, here's what happened." Bruce stood by a side window.

The window was broken into jagged shards. Pieces of glass lay scattered all over the floor. Klaus must have jumped through the window during the night and slashed himself open. He had barked as long as he'd had the strength.

"We can roll him onto this blanket and carry him out to the jeep," Alex said. He picked up the blanket off the sofa. To his surprise, his blue high school track shirt was lying under it. He must have left it here when he'd been sleeping on the sofa those first few days at Red Roof Farm. He rolled it in a ball and stuck it under his arm. Alex had learned that Bruce didn't have much curiosity about anything that didn't concern him directly, but even Bruce might be curious about the shirt and ask questions. And Alex didn't want to answer any questions right now.

Alex gave the room a quick once-over. Everything was just the way he had last seen it, except the plants, which were brown and withered. If they weren't already dead, they didn't have long to go. Well, the plants were the least of his problems.

Luckily Bruce was too busy examining Klaus's wounds to notice anything. "He'll never pull through. Why don't I shoot him now and get it over with?"

Alex knew that as long as Klaus lived he was a threat. Still, Alex remembered how Klaus had come running in answer to his whistle, slept at the foot of his bed, gone swimming with him. Klaus had been his loyal companion and Alex couldn't bring himself to let Bruce kill him.

"If we get him back into his cage, we can bandage him up and maybe he'll make it," Alex said.

Bruce shrugged. "It's your funeral."

It wasn't until Alex spread the blanket on the floor that he saw it was covered with long white cat hairs. It was as if a cat had been recently sleeping on it. The hairs were, in fact, just like the white cat hairs he'd noticed on the window seat in the big house. And they hadn't been on the blanket when Alex had first used it. He was sure of that.

Alex felt as if he'd been kicked in the gut as he and Bruce rolled Klaus onto the blanket. Klaus had patrolled this cottage those nights Alex had slept here, but he had never tried to get in. But tonight Klaus had risked his life to break in. Something had lured him in. A white Persian cat. It was the same white cat that had diverted Klaus from his attack on Alex yesterday afternoon. That was no sheet of polyethylene, no matter what Bruce thought, and polyethylene didn't scream like a cat either.

The white Persian cat had been shot and killed by the Baron last May. It didn't matter. Alex could no longer kid himself. The Baron and the Baroness and the cat might be gone, but their power here at Red Roof Farm had somehow clearly transcended their deaths.

Sixteen...

Alex and Bruce got Klaus in his cage, bandaged him up, gave him food and water, and left him alone. He slept for two days. On the third day, he began to act as if he were going to make it. Alex had mixed emotions. In one way, he wanted Klaus to live, but in another, he knew that, alive, the dog posed a constant danger to him.

Things were ominously quiet those three days. The air almost crackled with energy and tension as if an electrical storm were brewing, and it kept Alex on edge. On the fourth day of Klaus's recovery, Alex tried to keep busy by working around the yard while Bruce drove into town for supplies. Lately, Bruce used the Mercedes for everything. To be fair, Alex had to admit he kept it in great condition and waxed, polished and even vacuumed it just like the Baron probably had.

Alex was trimming along the front driveway when Bruce returned. They unloaded the car together. Bruce's biceps bulged as he lifted out a case of beer. Alex's track coach must have been putting them on when he told the team that beer made you flabby. Bruce drank beer all day long and had the build of a weightlifter.

Alex picked up a twenty-five-pound sack of dog food and staggered into the house with it. As he dumped the sack on the kitchen floor, he thought for about the tenth time he should get rid of all those dead plants by the windows. Then he did a second take. The plants looked better. Lots of dead leaves drooped listlessly, but new green shoots sprouted on every plant. Though it was beyond his rational understanding, it somehow made sense that the plants should be reviving. Those plants had belonged to the Baroness. So had the cat. If Alex could concede that the power of the cat had saved his life, he could certainly concede that these plants were rallying through no effort of his.

Alex abruptly turned away from the windows. His hands were clammy wet and he felt shaken. That kind of thinking got him nowhere.

"So how about it?" Bruce asked.

"Huh?"

"I said I convinced the girls that Klaus was locked up. They're coming out tomorrow night for a cookout and I asked if you'd broil steaks on the new grill I bought today."

"Oh yeah, sure." Alex knew he should have been elated that he was going to see Joanna again, but he couldn't seem to put his mind even to that as he helped Bruce put away the groceries.

The next day was one of those perfect, once-in-a-summer days with a bright sun, high blue skies and an occasional marshmallow cloud drifting by. Joanna and Sherrie were late, which was probably just as well. Alex had fallen asleep watching a ball game on TV and Bruce hadn't set up the new grill yet. By the time the girls arrived, the grill was at least ready, but the pool still needed cleaning and the kitchen was a mess.

Alex and Bruce were in the backyard when they heard the VW horn blaring out front. Bruce was lounging by the pool with a beer, watching Alex strain debris out of the water. They looked at each other as the honking continued. They were obviously being paged, and sure enough, when they came around the driveway, they saw the purple VW parked in front of the house with the girls still inside.

Sherrie rolled down her window and stuck out her head. "We're not stepping out of this car until you promise that dog is safely locked up."

Bruce laughed. "I forgot to tell you he's made an amazing recovery, escaped, and is lying in wait for you two juicy morsels."

Joanna laughed as she opened her door and got out. "Alex, where's your mustache?" she cried as soon as she saw him.

To cover up his embarrassment, Alex took off his glasses and wiped them on his shirt. He'd finally shaved off his mustache this morning when he realized it wasn't getting anywhere. Still, he was pleased that Joanna had noticed. And he was pleased to see Joanna's bare feet. He knew he shouldn't care that she was taller than he in clogs, but he was glad she wasn't wearing them today. The sun gleamed through her hair, turning it amber.

Sherrie was still in the car. Bruce leaned in her window, whispered something, then bent down and kissed her. That was all right with Alex. Maybe it would give Joanna ideas. But she wasn't watching. She was picking something out of the grass. A four-leaf clover.

"I think my luck's changed already," Alex said, taking her hand.

But Joanna pulled away and started running. "Since you're such a great track star, I'll race you to the pool," she called over her shoulder.

Alex took off after her, not even trying very hard. But as soon as he drew alongside, she put on more speed. He couldn't believe it. He ran as fast as he could but they were already across the driveway and almost to the pool before he passed her.

"Where did you last run, Madison Square Garden?" Alex sank down in a chair to catch his breath.

Joanna laughed but she was panting too. "Surprised you, didn't I? I'm the fastest forward on our field hockey team."

Alex had never much liked girl jocks before but, somehow, knowing Joanna was a good athlete appealed to him. He pretended not to watch as she unzipped her cut-offs and slid them down over her long legs. She wore the same green bikini as last time, but she must have been lying in the sun these past couple of days because she was more tanned. And the way she stood with her back to the lowering sun, a fine outline of golden hairs shone all over her body like a pale halo. She looked up and saw Alex studying her. Instead of blushing and pulling down her bikini or adjusting her straps like 99 percent of the girls Alex knew would do, she just grinned. All of a sudden, Alex felt good. Not just good, great.

He stood up and peeled off his own shirt and pants. For the first time in a long while he didn't feel self-conscious about his hairless chest or his ribs sticking out. He dropped his clothes on the table, opened the cooler and took out two beers.

Joanna shook her head. "I don't want a beer."

"Actually I don't want one either. I'll get us some Cokes." Alex started up the driveway toward the house.

"Hey, Alex, get the camera, will you? We never finished taking pictures last time," Sherrie shouted after him. She and Bruce had come around the side of the house hand in hand.

"It's in the den," Bruce called.

Alex waved a yes and took the back steps four at a time. He just knew it was going to be a perfect evening. As he headed for the refrigerator for the Coke, he made a special effort not to look at the plants in the window. Nothing, absolutely nothing, was going to spoil his good time with Joanna tonight. He got the Coke, then, at a trot, he headed for the den. As always, the den was dark. Alex turned on a light, but he didn't see the camera. It wasn't on the desk, the coffee table, the sofa, or the top of the TV. Maybe Bruce had put it in the desk.

Alex still felt strange about the desk, with its silent, waiting typewriter and the jagged bullet hole head-level in the wall. He mentally braced himself as he began to open drawers, first the wide middle one, then each side drawer in turn. But he didn't see the camera. If it was anywhere, it was probably in the big bottom drawer. It wasn't in there either. But a piece of blank paper he hadn't noticed before was propped up against one end.

Maybe it was behind that. He lifted the paper.

To Alex's surprise, the camera *was* behind the paper. He reached down and lifted it out. Then he heard a snuffing sound like a snore. As he started into the drawer, he realized the sound had come from him. Under the camera was a metal cat lying on top of two books. It was the cat medallion that the Baroness had worn in every one of her photographs. And it was exactly like the Roman-looking cat she used to sign her paintings. Only this medallion wasn't a photograph or a signature or a carved wooden key label. It was the real thing. It was about two inches high and of some kind of metal—gold Alex guessed—with small, green-jewel eyes that seemed to be staring right up at him.

Alex's first reaction was to slam the drawer shut. But the unblinking green eyes were like a magnet pulling on him. Against his every instinct, Alex reached down and picked up the medallion and two books. The medallion was surprisingly heavy. It was crudely made, almost primitive, and the green eyes were rough, uncut jewels. He turned the medallion over. Initials and a date were engraved on the back, "A. L. V. 1889."

Alex put the medallion down on the desk and reluctantly picked up the first book. The title was *Handbook for Everyday Law*, with subtitles listed on the cover: *Contracts, Real Property, Partnerships, Mortgages, Wills, Divorce, Copyrights, Sales*. It meant nothing to Alex. Neither did the second book. It was some kind of leather notebook filled with handwritten lists and notes and outlines, obviously written by different people at different times. Some of the ink was brown and faded, and some was black and new. It didn't matter. It was all in a foreign language that Alex couldn't read. German.

Four or five official-looking typewritten blue airmail letters addressed to the Baroness here at Red Roof Farm were stuck in the back cover of the notebook. Alex quickly glanced over them. They were in German too. Wait a minute. At the bottom of one of the letters was a hand-drawn picture of a cat, not exactly like the cat medallion, but close enough so Alex was sure that was what it referred to.

All of a sudden, a whole lot of things became clear. Finding the camera on top of the cat medallion and these books was some kind of signal. It was a signal, like finding the Libertas Cottage key on the Mercedes dashboard after none of the cars would start had been a signal leading him to the cottage. Just the fact he even knew the cottage existed had been a signal. Alex remembered that bright flash of light that had attracted his attention to the cottage the day he and Dad had arrived. And that yellow scarf fluttering out the Baron's closet door had been a signal too, leading him to find all that Nazi material. And what about the plants and insulin? Signals, all of them, telling him the Baroness's spirit, force or whatever it was, wanted something of him.

Could that be why Klaus had attacked him? Yes, it was possible. When Alex's mind was closed to the signals, Klaus was his friend and companion, but the moment Alex had acknowledged the Baroness's signals, Klaus had turned against him. And that was a Klaus under orders. Klaus was as inseparable from the Baron, dead or not, as the white cat was inseparable from the Baroness. Twice that cat had saved Alex, and now he knew why.

He had been saved for some definite purpose. And he was sure that purpose had to do with these books and letters. They were important, terribly important. The very presence of the cat medallion told him that. He was meant to do something with them. Find out what was in them. Act on them.

All of a sudden, Alex was suffocating. The dark den pressed in on him from every side and he could hardly breathe. Terrifying factions he couldn't see were demanding something of him he didn't understand. He couldn't handle it. He *wouldn't* handle it. He'd have nothing to do with any of this.

Alex threw the medallion and the books back into the drawer and slammed it shut. He picked up the camera and raced out the side patio door. But, in his rush, the blood must have drained from his head. He was so dizzy he had to grab a chair to steady himself as a vast roar filled his ears and his vision blurred.

Seventeen...

"Hey, Alex!"

Dimly Alex realized someone was calling him. He tried to focus on where the voice had come from. There, it was Bruce, down by the barn. He was polishing the Mercedes while Sherrie watched.

Still dizzy, Alex started across the backyard, carefully putting one foot in front of the other as if he were walking a tightrope.

"What took you so long?" Bruce sounded angry.

"It was the camera . . . I had to look everywhere for it . . ."

"Oh Bruce, let's get some pictures of the Mercedes before we take it out." Sherrie put her hand on Bruce's shoulder and gave it a squeeze.

"We're going out in the Mercedes?" That must be why Bruce was in such a foul mood. The Mercedes was Bruce's private property and he didn't like sharing it with anyone. Well, Alex was in a foul mood too, and he had a lot more on his mind than a Mercedes.

"We're only driving into town and back." Bruce made it clear it wasn't his idea.

"I want to go past George Duffy's garage so some of

the idiots there can see me in it." Sherrie pulled out a brush and began to brush her hair.

Alex remembered Joanna mentioning something about George Duffy being Sherrie's ex-boyfriend. Joanna. He didn't see her anywhere.

"Where's Joanna?" he asked.

"She's down with that crazy dog," Sherrie said. "Here, give me the camera, Alex, so Bruce and me can get some pictures."

Alex handed the camera to Sherrie and started around the side of the barn toward the kennels.

"Joanna?"

She was crouched down by Klaus's cage. Her long hair was soaking wet and so was the outline of her bikini under her shirt as if she had just been swimming. Klaus, lying on his side next to the wiring, was licking her fingers. His tail thumped happily. Then he saw Alex. His ears went up and a growl started deep in his chest.

Joanna's eyebrows formed questioning arcs. "What's with you and this dog? He and I were doing fine until you showed up."

Everyone was in a bad mood. Their great evening was going down the tubes. "I beat him every chance I get," Alex retorted.

Klaus had worked himself up to a half-sitting position, but the exertion must have opened his wounds again. Fresh blood stained his bandages. He tried to bark, but didn't have the strength. Alex stared at the dog. Klaus was wasting his energy. Alex was no threat to Klaus, the Baron, or anyone else. He was through with messages, signals, cat medallions, books, letters. Now and forever. In fact, all he wanted to do was forget the whole thing. He reached down, took Joanna's hand and pulled her to her feet.

"Come on, we're going for a ride in the Mercedes."

Sherrie was posing against the front fender of the car while Bruce focused the lens. He was frowning. "Hey, Alex, I took only two pictures last time by the pool but today the film is on number six. Were you fooling with it?"

"No."

"Huh, well, maybe I rolled the film too far."

Alex was astounded. He had never heard Bruce admit to a mistake before about anything.

They took lots of pictures, pictures of Sherrie and Bruce, Joanna and Alex, Sherrie and Joanna—every combination they could think of—until the film was used up. Bruce opened the camera, took out the film and handed it to Sherrie.

"Have your father's store develop these, will you?"

Sherrie shoved the roll in her pocket. "Yeah, and I'll get more film so we can take pictures at the party."

So the costume party was still on. That was too bad. Alex climbed in the back seat. Joanna started to get in beside him but Bruce grabbed her. "Where do you think you're going all wet like that?"

"I'm not wet."

"You are too. Get some towels to sit on."

Joanna glared at Bruce, then ran up to the pool and came back with a couple of towels and Alex's shirt. "Mr. Fusspot," she muttered as she flopped on the back seat next to Alex.

Things were going from bad to worse. That four-leaf clover had been some good luck. Alex tried to ease the tension. "You just have to understand that the Mercedes is Bruce's baby."

Bruce had already started the motor. He shifted into first and released the brake.

"Bruce must be German. Only a German could love a car the way he does." Joanna sounded uncharacteristically snappish.

"You don't like Germans?"

"Are you kidding? With a name like Joanna Hebbel, I *am* German. At least as German as an American can be. Mom's family has been here for two generations, but Dad left Germany with his parents when he was eight to escape Hitler."

Now they were rounding the corner of the house, the diesel engine purring loudly. Alex was making every effort to relax, but Joanna's talk about her German family sent him right back to that desk drawer and those books and letters in German. He had to force himself back to the conversation. "So your mother was born in Germany?"

"No, I said my father is German. Not that my mother's family isn't German too. Can you imagine, her parents have lived in Milwaukee practically forever and still speak almost nothing but German?"

One half of Alex was aware of the sweep of cool air as Bruce turned on the air conditioning and the other half heard what Joanna said. Immediately he rejected it, refused even to consider it. Instead, he leaned forward and spoke to Sherrie. "You really dig this car, don't you, Sherrie?"

She turned around and her smile was so broad both cheeks dimpled. "I never enjoyed anything so much in my life. Their Royal Highnesses the Von Dursts used to drive around in this Mercedes with their noses a mile in the air." Sherrie giggled. "Now I'm riding in it. I can't believe it."

They passed over the last traffic bump in the driveway and Bruce shifted into third. It was a beautiful car. It was a beautiful day. The girls were beautiful. Alex should have been having the time of his life. Instead, he was miserable. And he knew why. He might as well ask Joanna and get it over with.

"With your German relatives and all, I bet your German is as bad as my Spanish." He made it a statement so she wouldn't have to answer.

But she reacted right away. "Are you serious? I'm fluent in German. In fact, I'm taking fourth-year Honors German next year. I might as well cash in on what I already know."

"You can read German?"

Joanna looked puzzled. "Of course. Why?"

Joanna could translate those German letters and the notebook! A half groan escaped Alex's lips before he could stop it. "No reason," he mumbled. "Forget it."

...Eighteen

Alex backed the pickup out of the barn and started up the driveway. The muffler sounded worse than ever, like something out of a drag race. As he passed Bruce and Sherrie sitting by the pool, Bruce signaled him to stop.

"Make an appointment to get that muffler fixed," Bruce yelled.

"And tell Joanna to show you the pictures we took. They turned out real good," Sherrie added.

Alex saluted an okay and took off. He wanted to pick up speed and get some air circulating. It was about 95° out and humid too. He and Joanna planned to go to an air-conditioned movie in town. They'd turned down a big beer blast of a picnic that Sherrie and Bruce were going to later. He and Joanna had a better time alone, plus Joanna was going away tomorrow for a trip through Virginia with family friends and they wouldn't see each other for five days. Not only that but thunderclouds were rolling in from the west, heavy with the threat of rain ruining the picnic.

The past week had been heavy with more than just

the weather. The knowledge that Joanna could translate the German notebook and letters he'd found in the desk weighed Alex down like a millstone. They were important, he knew that, but he had made up his mind not to show them to her. He had counted on being on his own this summer, free from his parents' nagging, free of teachers telling him what to do, free of everything. And he wasn't going to let anything spoil that for him. The books and letters still lay in the desk drawer where he had left them.

So why did he avoid asking Joanna out to Red Roof Farm? Both times Sherrie had come to visit Bruce, Alex had made an excuse to see Joanna in town. Alex didn't even have to ask himself the question because he already knew the answer. He didn't trust himself not to show Joanna the notebook and letters, and he didn't want to know what was in them. He refused to know. They were trouble. They meant getting involved in something he had no intention of getting involved in. Alex calculated the summer. It was now almost half over. Well, he'd made it this far, he'd just have to hang in there and make it through the rest.

Alex turned right toward town at the end of the driveway. Sweat formed all around the rims of his glasses. He took them off and wiped them on a rag he kept under the seat, and wiped his face at the same time. Plenty of air was coming in, but it was all hot.

Alex shifted into third to take the long sloping hill into town. He was really learning to handle a four-wheel drive pretty well. He braked at the stop sign at the bottom, but a big truck blocked his way at the corner. As he started to pass it, he realized it was a garbage truck. A garbage truck was what Red Roof Farm needed more than anything. Alex pulled over to the side of the road and jumped out.

Two men were emptying garbage cans into the truck's grinding maw.

Alex greeted them. "Hi, are you Malone's Disposal?"

One of them looked up. "Yeah, I'm Ed Malone."

"I'm taking care of Red Roof Farm this summer out on Terrill Road. We've been bagging and stacking garbage for weeks and it's really raunchy. I've called you a couple of times and left a message with your answering service, but you never called back. Can you make a pickup?"

Ed Malone shrugged. "My answering service does a lousy job. I never got your message. Yeah, I could swing around out there this week, I guess." His florid face was flushed almost crimson with the heat. "Red Roof Farm. That's where those people got killed, huh? That lady cancelled us last May."

That was a surprise. "The lady cancelled you in May?"

Ed Malone pulled out a handkerchief and mopped his face, but all he did was smear the dirt around. "Yeah, she asked me and Mac here to sign some papers as a favor. Then she gave us ten dollars each and said not to come back, that she wanted twice a week service and was going to hire RBS Disposal outta Clarkston."

"Signed a paper?" Alex was beginning to sound like an echo.

"You know, like witnesses. She signed the paper, then Mac signed it, then I signed it. It was no big deal.

She said it was some kind of contract that needed witnesses."

"Did you see what it was?"

"Nah."

"Well, I did." Mac spoke up for the first time. "It was typed, but it was in a foreign language I couldn't read. You know, like French."

"Thanks."

Alex mulled it over as he headed back to the pickup. A contract? In German? He couldn't imagine what it could have been. He waved his thanks as he pulled around the truck, the roar of his muffler louder than ever.

Alex met Joanna at the store and waited while she locked up. Then they drove to Fallsboro to the movies. But Alex was so distracted by his encounter with the garbagemen, he hardly saw the picture. At least the theater was cool, and by the time they stopped for hamburgers and had driven back to Wye Mills, Alex felt better. He was making a monumental effort to push the whole Ed Malone witnessing-a-contract business out of his mind. Besides, Joanna knew how to kid him out of a bad mood, just the way he knew how to tease her out of a bad mood too. They meshed well together.

Alex walked Joanna up to her front door. A blue half-light shone through the porch window and Alex saw Mr. Osborne asleep on the couch in front of the flickering TV. He decided not to go in.

"Goodnight, Joanna." He leaned forward, put his arms around her and kissed her, gently at first, then harder. He felt the thin film of perspiration on her upper lip and tasted the faintly salty flavor of it. She pressed against him and kissed him back. All of a sudden, she pulled away and laughed.

"What's so funny?" Alex knew he wasn't the greatest kisser in the world, but he didn't think he was the worst either.

"I just got my braces off last month. This is the best kiss I ever had."

Another link between them. "I had braces until last year too. We might have been locked together for life." It *was* pretty funny.

"Thanks for the movie and I'll see you next week." Joanna gave Alex a quick kiss and a farewell hug.

"Good-bye, Joanna, and have fun." Alex reached for her again, but she had already opened the door and slipped inside.

Alex thought about Joanna all the way home. Because he liked her better every time he saw her, he hated the thought of not seeing her for five days. Why couldn't Sherrie have gone and Joanna stayed home? It was strange to think the two girls were cousins. They certainly were nothing alike. Alex turned into the Red Roof Farm driveway. It was still unbelievably hot, with no moon or stars. It was as if the smothering blanket of heat had extinguished all light. His shirt stuck to the seat cover and even his headlights only penetrated to the edge of the woods. A couple of times he heard distant thunder and saw a brief flash of lightning. That was all right with him. A good storm might clear the air.

As Alex drove out of the woods into the clearing, he noticed right away the house was completely dark. A monstrous shadow in the night, it seemed transfixed in time and space, as if it had taken root and would stand there forever. Alex slowed down as he drove around the driveway. For sure, the back would be lit up. He and Bruce always left the house ablaze. But the back was as dark as the front. The empty eye sockets of windows gaped black. Alex's mind ricocheted from one course of action to another. In the end, he just kept going. His headlights lit up the barn. The jeep was in place, but the Mercedes was gone. Bruce and Sherrie must have left for the picnic before dark and forgotten to turn on any lights.

Even with that sensible explanation, Alex's heart was thudding against his ribs as he reached in the glove compartment for the flashlight. When he turned it on, he realized the battery must be almost dead. He started up the driveway with only a pale circle of yellow to guide his way.

He was halfway to the house when an unearthly wail stopped him in his tracks. The wild plaint hung suspended in the still air, then faded. All that was left in the silence was the sound of Alex's breath wheezing in and out. It was Klaus. Alex knew that, and he knew too that Klaus was safely locked up. Nevertheless, the hairs on the back of his neck prickled.

Alex gripped the flashlight and took long, measured steps up the driveway, forcing himself not to panic. He had never been aware before that the drive was so steeply angled, but by the time he reached the back porch, he had to stop and wait for his heart to slow down. He unlocked the back door and turned on the hall light switch. Click. Now for the kitchen. Just as he reached for the kitchen light, a boom of thunder clapped overhead, followed in seconds by a dazzling flash of lightning that captured everything in place like a flashbulb exploding in the dark. Alex's knees almost gave out from under him.

"Shape up. Get in control," he told himself as he turned on the pantry light and pushed open the swinging door into the dining room. He wouldn't even bother with the dining room light. He'd just get through fast and into the living room. Though he had long ago taken down the linens and table setting, the dining room still bugged him as if two people in red costumes were about to enter and sit down for their formal evening meal.

There, he made it through the dining room. But the nearest living room light was the lamp over by the fireplace. Crrraaacck! Another slam of thunder shook the house, followed immediately by lightning. The storm was right overhead. Still the rain didn't come.

Alex had already started across the dark living room when he smelled smoke. Cigarette smoke. He kept walking, but he was breathing so hard he knew he was close to hyperventilating. Now he heard the slap of rain on the tile roof and against the windows coming in from the west. He was hardly aware of it. Smoke. Someone in the house was smoking. He was too stunned to shift gears and run. He was too stunned to do anything but what he had started out to do, turn on the light.

But before he could reach the lamp, another crack of thunder exploded, followed by instant lightning. At that moment, he glanced up at the mirror above the fireplace. In the brief second of vivid white light, he clearly and distinctly saw two figures reflected in the mirror, poised on the stair landing behind him. One was tall and heavy in an officer's black uniform. The other was small and thin, her red satin dress shimmering in the shadows, and the tip of her cigarette a red glow.

...Nineteen

It never occurred to Alex to run. Or even move. Nothing occurred to him at all. Little throbs of fear pulsed in his throat and, for some reason, in the far distance, he heard Klaus still barking. That was real. What he had seen in the mirror wasn't.

The rain was heavy on the roof now, splashing down the drains. Without any conscious decision on his part, Alex slowly turned to face the stair landing. Only the pantry light was on, its narrow beam poking long-fingered shadows into the living room. The two figures were still on the landing, just standing there. Then the woman took the man's arm, and without a word, they started down the stairs together.

"No . . . no . . ."

It was barely a whisper and Alex had uttered it. Now the pair had reached the bottom of the stairs. The man silently raised his hand to his hip, pulled a revolver from his holster and pointed it at Alex. A revolver! For the first time, Alex connected one thought to another. It was the Von Dursts, and the Baron was going to kill him. Still Alex couldn't move. He had nowhere to go. All that was left were words.

"Leave me alone! I don't want anything to do with you!" he shouted.

It was all he could do. Now it was over. No one would ever know what had happened to him. The rain drummed a loud heartbeat on the roof.

Alex tensed every muscle, squeezed his eyes shut and waited. Nothing. He slit his eyes open a fraction. The woman's hands covered her face and she was making gasping noises as if she were crying. The man lowered his gun and put his arm around her. They leaned against each other, their shoulders shaking. They weren't crying. They were laughing. Laughing! Their laughter resounded through Alex's head like echoing laughter in a tunnel of horrors. Then, through his numbness, some form of reasoning process resumed. He recognized something familiar, known.

Wham! Another shock of thunder hit, farther away this time, but still followed by the white streak of lightning. This time Alex saw more than he had last time. He saw, not the Baroness's gray hair and heavy arms, but shiny black hair and a slender figure, and not an old man's stooped silhouette, but broad young shoulders and slim hips in the black uniform.

Alex reached behind him and turned on the light, sure of what he would see. Bruce and Sherrie. They were laughing so hard they were almost doubled over. Black mascara tracks ran down Sherrie's face and Bruce coughed and sputtered, trying to catch his breath.

"I . . . never saw anyone . . . so scared . . . ever . . ." Bruce could hardly get the words out.

In all his life Alex had never experienced anything like the rage that overwhelmed him at that moment.

With a snarl of fury, he sprang at Bruce, covering the distance between them in one leap. As he hit Bruce full force in the chest, he was aware of Bruce's strong beer breath and his white teeth bared in a grin. Then, as they crashed to the floor, Bruce's face went slack. He must have hit his head. For a moment he lay motionless. Alex was beyond control or knowing what he was doing. He began to pound Bruce on the chest, the shoulders, the arms.

"You bastard . . . you bastard . . . you bastard . . ." He had no idea what he was saying.

Then Bruce began to struggle against him. With a powerful shove, he pushed Alex off. But Alex had a death grip. Together they rolled over and over on the floor, first one on top, then the other. Then Alex was straddling Bruce. He grabbed for Bruce's throat. Vaguely he realized Sherrie was screaming and pounding him on the back with her fists.

Whop! Alex saw bright lights burst in a black field. Something heavy had cracked him on the back of the head. His hands around Bruce's throat went limp and he slumped back on his heels, fighting the inclination to pass out.

Bruce rolled out from under him, rubbing his throat. He wasn't laughing now. He was ashen under his tan. "My God . . . you coulda killed me."

Dazed, Alex looked behind him. Someone in a red dress holding a brass candlestick leaned over him. She must have used it to hit him on the head. But he couldn't piece together what had happened. The red satin dress . . . the Nazi uniform . . . the Von Dursts . . . the

Baron had tried to kill him . . . no, it was Bruce and Sherrie . . .

"It was only a joke, you fool!" Sherrie spit the words out as she dropped the candlestick and ran over to Bruce.

Alex smelled liquor on her breath too. They were drunk. They had to be drunk to pull a stunt like that. But how had they guessed turning off the lights and posing as the Von Dursts was the one thing he couldn't handle?

"What were you doing? What made you do that?" Alex demanded.

Sherrie looked up from where she was comforting Bruce on the floor. Her face was streaked and dirty. "We were upstairs trying on clothes for the party when Joanna called to say she left her wallet in your pickup, so we knew you were on your way. When we heard your muffler, we turned out all the lights." Sherrie was getting madder and madder. "It was just a joke, you idiot!" she yelled again.

"But the Mercedes is gone."

Bruce pushed Sherrie away from him and took off his heavy wool uniform jacket. His T-shirt underneath was wet with sweat and Alex realized that Bruce was very drunk. "I hid the Mercedes behind the barn." His words were slurred.

Yes, Alex could see how it happened. They hadn't been prompted or programmed to do it. It was all just a coincidence and they had no idea of the hell he'd been going through this past week.

"Heart attack time, huh, Alex? 'Leave me alone. I

don't want anything to do with you.' " Bruce imitated Alex in a high falsetto. "You can't say we didn't scare you outta your skull." Bruce sounded grimly pleased as he stood up and brushed off his pants. Then he reached for Sherrie's hand.

"C'mon, I need a cold beer."

Alex watched the two of them walk through the dining room and into the pantry. He was suddenly so exhausted he could barely make it to a chair. Out in the kitchen he heard Bruce say something then laugh. Sherrie answered in a lower voice. The rain had let up some, but still tapped against the windows. Klaus's frantic barking had quieted too.

Alex rubbed his head and felt a raised bump. It wasn't bad and there was no blood. In a way, he was glad it hurt. It helped him stay alert and he needed to be alert. He had avoided things long enough. Now he had to come to terms with them. He laid his head back and closed his eyes.

"I don't want anything to do with you."

Alex had said that. Distinctly, consciously, and he had meant it. He had rejected doing what had to be done because he was afraid. More than afraid. Panicked. Bruce and Sherrie had no idea why he had been so terrified of their masquerade and they never would. At least he would never tell them. Even if they knew, they wouldn't care. They both wore blinders to everyone and everything but themselves. But he didn't have blinders. He knew what was going on and had refused to get involved.

This was a matter of murder. The Baron had murdered his wife, and right now, for the first time, Alex was sure he had killed her for some very definite reason that had nothing to do with a love pact like everyone thought. And Alex had been pressured through signals, messages, portents—every kind of means there was—to find that reason. It was the authority of the Baroness demanding help from him and he could no longer deny it. And just as clearly, he knew the iron determination of the Baron was trying to stop him.

They had been Nazis, both of them, and deserved everything they got. It had been as good an excuse as any for Alex not to get involved. But that excuse no longer worked. Alex opened his eyes. Only one light was on, but it was enough to see by. The oil portraits glared down at him from every wall. They were telling him to stay away, get out, put on the blinders and stick with Bruce. But Alex had tried that and he couldn't live with it. He stared back at the portraits defiantly. The time had come to take a stand. It was a risk, he knew that, and he was still scared. But he had to do it. Yes, he'd put that medallion and the books and letters in his room for safekeeping. Then as soon as Joanna got back from her trip, he would ask her to translate them.

...Twenty

The day of the costume party broke with a thick haze hovering in the air. Alex looked out the kitchen window. He could usually get an idea of the weather by studying the mountains in the distance to the east. Sometimes the mountains jumped out at him, but today they receded into a misty vapor. As Alex turned on the radio for the morning weather report, he glanced down at the Baroness's plants. Lots of new yellow-green shoots pushed up between the brown stalks.

Alex didn't kid himself. These plants didn't have anything to do with his watering or not watering. They had been doing well this week, ever since he had decided to let Joanna translate those letters and notebook for him. The trouble was, Joanna was still away. She had extended her trip to Virginia an extra two days and wasn't due back until today, just in time to come out to Red Roof Farm for the party.

Alex opened the refrigerator and pushed aside a carton of Coke to get a peach from the back shelf. He hadn't thought about the bottle of insulin for days, but now he saw it was almost empty. All of a sudden, Alex realized this insulin bottle was like an hour glass with the sand running out. It was as if the Baroness were telling him that her time was almost up.

Alex felt totally frustrated. Though he had been over everything again and again, it was like trying to fit a jigsaw puzzle together in the dark. He knew all the pieces were there, but he couldn't connect one disjointed segment to another. The only concrete material he had to work with were the books and letters he'd found in the desk. He had to know what was in them. Today. If only it rained and the party were postponed, he could drive to Wye Mills, see Joanna this afternoon, and settle this once and for all.

Alex tossed his peach pit in the wastebasket just as Bruce shuffled into the kitchen still half asleep. He rubbed the hair on his chest and yawned.

"It looks like rain," Alex said.

"Yeah, well, plans are changed. The band's got a gig in Harrisburg tomorrow night so the party's on, rain or no rain."

Alex didn't answer. Ever since that lowdown masquerade prank, things had changed between Alex and Bruce. They got along okay, but didn't have any more to do with each other than was necessary. It was as if an invisible toe mark had been drawn between them that neither wanted to cross. Alex took another peach from the refrigerator and headed outside.

Bruce was on a real high all day. Alex had never seen him work so hard. About a hundred kids were coming to the party, each paying a $4 entrance fee. That still didn't cover expenses. Even at a discount through Mr. Osborne, the food and beer cost over $200 and the Innocent Bystanders Band was charging $300. Without

131 • • •

even discussing it, Bruce had billed everything to the Von Durst Estate account. Dad would have a fit when he saw the bills, but Alex had already voiced his opinion about the party and wasn't going to say anything more.

Bruce was a good handyman and he'd put together some kind of makeshift platform for the band on the patio, hooked up loudspeakers, and even rented outdoor floodlights and installed them. Alex was a hopeless mechanic. As soon as he shorted one of the floodlights, Bruce had assigned him the yard work and setting up. He started by trimming the grass around the pool. Every time he went past Klaus's cage with a load for the compost pile, the dog threw himself against the wires in a frenzy. It was as if Klaus sensed the deadline were up too.

The rain held off, but as the day went on the sky changed. It looked not better, but different. A yellowish vapor, like industrial pollution, hung low and the mountains in the east disappeared entirely in the sulfurous haze. Bruce was getting edgy. There had been no word from the band, though they had said they would phone for directions. Everything else was ready. Alex had set up rented tables around the backyard, with two half-kegs of beer at either end of the pool.

The girls were due to arrive at six, but didn't show up until seven. Joanna climbed out of the VW first, loaded down with two huge pickle jars. Alex grabbed them from her and set them on one of the tables as Bruce helped Sherrie unload food from the trunk.

"Hey, Joanna," Alex said in a low voice. He didn't know when he had ever been so glad to see anyone. He knew he was grinning from ear to ear like an idiot. Joanna was grinning too. He reached out and gave her a hard hug and she hugged him back. She felt wiry and strong in his arms and it was nice.

Then everything was confusion. Sherrie's father, in a burst of generosity, had donated a vat of potato salad that had turned over in the back seat. No one could open the pickle jars, one of the table legs collapsed, and Klaus kept up his barking until Alex thought he'd go mad with it. Then, just when everything was finally in order, the Innocent Bystanders' van pulled up in a blaze of honking horns and screeching brakes.

Alex had never seen so much equipment. As he watched the band plug in their instruments, he was sure they'd blow every fuse in the place. But that wasn't Alex's problem. He had enough of his own. All he wanted right now was to show Joanna the letters and notebook. But first he'd better hide the car keys and lock the barn before anyone arrived. He took the car keys back to the house, gathered up the rest of the keys from the back hall and hid them all in the laundry room. He might only be a high school junior, but he knew what went on at parties.

He found Joanna and Sherrie working in the kitchen. Joanna had on a green blouse and a wrap-around skirt and he realized it was the first time he had ever seen her in a skirt. And she'd had her hair cut. Usually she wore it in a ponytail or parted in the middle and swept behind her ears, but now it was short and curled up at the ends. Alex wasn't sure whether he liked it or not. She was slicing onions at the sink when he came up behind her.

"You've got to come with me for a minute," he whispered. Sherrie stood at the kitchen table unwrapping hot-dog rolls.

Joanna turned around. Her eyes were red and full of

tears. Even her nose was running. "Let me finish these onions first."

"Sherrie can do them."

"Sherrie hates onions."

Alex could understand why. Sherrie was her usual spectacular self in a black blouse and tight slacks, but her face looked plasticized with makeup. Slicing onions would probably unglue her altogether.

"Then do them later." Onions! Who cared about onions? Alex took Joanna's hand and led her from the kitchen. As soon as they were in the pantry, he reached up and touched her hair. It was springy and thick. "I like your hair," he said and as soon as he said it, he realized he did like it.

"So what do you want?" Joanna wiped her still-red eyes.

Alex took her into the den without answering. He had already brought the books and letters down and stuck them under a chair cushion for safekeeping. The cat medallion was in his pocket. He plunked Joanna down on the sofa and handed her the notebook.

"This book is all in German. I want you to translate it and I especially want you to translate the letters in the back." Alex sounded calm, but his heart was thumping somewhere up in his throat. From outside, the Innocent Bystanders were beginning to warm up in a discordant cacophony of electrical whines and squawks.

In turn, Joanna reached into her skirt pocket and handed Alex a yellow Kodak envelope. "Here are the pictures we took. I keep forgetting to show them to you."

Alex could have cared less about the pictures, but he

glanced over them for something to do. They were the pictures of the four of them with the Mercedes. Though they were all laughing and smiling, Alex remembered what a rotten mood everyone had been in that day. It seemed like a million years ago. And there were three pictures he didn't recognize that must have already been on the film. They weren't very good, but right away he realized all three were of the Baroness's bird painting in Libertas Cottage. One photograph showed only the painting. One was taken farther back so part of the sofa was included. The third picture showed the entire sofa and the painting too. They were blurry and out of focus, but something more than that was peculiar about them. Alex studied them one at a time, but couldn't figure out what it was that bothered him.

"This is some kind of genealogy." Joanna interrupted his train of thought.

"You mean like who's related to whom?" Alex slipped the photographs in his hip pocket.

"Yes, it goes back to seventeen-something. The ink is so faint I can't read the early dates, but it's the Baron's genealogy. There's a page started for the Baroness, but it's blank."

That must mean something, but Alex couldn't imagine what. "Read the letters, especially the one with the picture of the cat." Maybe those would explain more.

"Hey, kid, where's some extension cords?"

It was the guitarist standing in the den doorway. His wild red hair and beard looked as if they had already been plugged in.

Alex waved him away. "I don't know. Ask Bruce."

Joanna picked up the first letter and began to read. Alex watched her run her finger slowly along the lines for a minute or two, but he was too impatient to stand still for long. He began to pace, from the glassed-in bookcases to the TV set to the door to the desk. The desk. He wondered if he would ever get used to the splintered bullet hole in the wall. The Baroness had been so real to him today, it took that bullet hole to bring him back to the reality of her death. She was dead, he had to remind himself of that. Dead, he thought, yet in a way, not dead. A shiver ran up his back.

From outside Alex heard car doors slamming, people shouting back and forth, the band beginning to play something that sounded like music, Bruce shouting at Sherrie to start collecting money and, above all the bedlam, the sound of Klaus barking. The party had begun.

Still Alex paced on, even when he heard Bruce calling to him to get the ice from the basement. What was taking Joanna so long? She was totally absorbed. Two exclamation lines furrowed her forehead. Then she put the letters down. She was biting her lip and staring blankly at the rug.

"Well?" Alex demanded.

Her head snapped up as if he had startled her. "Where did you get these letters?"

"It doesn't matter. I found them." As Alex glanced at Joanna, he realized she had tears in her eyes. Tears! It was too much. He grabbed her shoulders and began to shake her. "What's it about, Joanna? Tell me. I have to know."

Twenty-one...

Joanna's head jerked back and forth as Alex shook her again and again. "Stop it, Alex!" she shouted.

Embarrassed, Alex backed off. "I'm sorry, Joanna, but I have to know what's in those letters."

But Joanna wasn't about to be intimidated. "I'll tell you what's in them if you tell me what this is all about."

Blackmail. Still, fair was fair. "All right," Alex said, "but you go first."

Joanna looked suddenly serious. "The Von Dursts must have been doing their family genealogy. The Baroness wrote the town hall in Stuttgart, Germany, asking questions about her family history. They wrote back saying there was confusion over her records and they needed more information."

Joanna held up the second letter. "She must have sent them what they wanted because this next letter back says she was legally adopted in 1915 as an infant by Werner and Renate Schuller of Stuttgart."

So? Alex didn't see that adoption was such a big deal. Lots of people were adopted and, from the photographs in the album, the Baroness had done pretty well. The Schullers had plenty of money, a big house, a summer place on a lake, cars, horses, servants. In fact, they looked like your big, happy, all-around Nazi family.

But Joanna wasn't finished. "The Baroness must have been surprised she was adopted because the next letter from Stuttgart gives dates, hospital, and the name of her real mother, Anna Vogel, artist, now deceased. Father unknown."

From outside Alex heard a chorus of horns honking. A whole caravan of cars had arrived at the same time. The Innocent Bystanders were warmed up now and, even though the loudspeakers faced away from the house, it was hard to hear anything above their beat. Even the floor vibrated.

Joanna had to raise her voice. "The Baroness must have sent money to trace her mother because Stuttgart thanked her for the money order and said they would write her when the inquiry was complete. Then this last letter, months later, gives the whole story. This one, with the cat drawn on the bottom of it."

At last, at long last. In one way, Alex couldn't wait to hear. In another, he didn't want to hear anything. Once he knew, he would be in so deep there would be no way out. He walked over to the window and drew back the curtain. A pickup had just pulled up on the grass by the pool and a gang of kids was piling out. Only they weren't kids. They looked at least twenty-one or twenty-two and they looked like trouble. Well, this party was Bruce's big idea; let him handle it.

Alex mentally squared his shoulders. "Okay, Joanna, what's it say?"

"Anna Vogel was an artist. She was never married but lived with a man in Stuttgart, a sculptor, name unknown. After her daughter was born and adopted by the Schullers, Anna Vogel moved to Berlin where she lived for twenty-four years at various addresses. Then in 1940 she was interred in Buchenwald concentration camp. Her death was recorded there in 1944."

Joanna's eyes brimmed with tears again. But Alex was too shocked to notice. All he could think about were those photographs of the Baroness, every one with Nazi officers or officials. Her adopted family had all been Nazis too. For that matter so had the Baroness herself. And her real mother had died in a Nazi concentration camp!

"Hey, is there a john around here?"

Alex couldn't focus on the figure standing in the den doorway. It was a clown with an exaggerated grin painted on his face.

"A john," the clown repeated as if Alex weren't very bright.

Alex jerked his thumb toward the hall. "Upstairs."

Joanna got out of her chair and walked over to stand beside Alex. "What's this all about? You promised to tell me. Do you think the Baroness shot herself when she found out how her mother died?"

"Maybe." No, wait. Alex glanced back at the desk and the gaping hole in the wall. The Baroness had been shot through the back of the head. She couldn't have killed herself. He was sure of that, but he wasn't sure of anything else. "What's the date of that last letter?" he asked.

"May nineteenth."

May 19 was ten days before the killings. It had probably taken that long for the letter to get here from

Germany. The two events must be connected. Alex started to pace again. "What does the letter say about the cat?"

Joanna picked up the letter with the cat and glanced over it. "When the Baroness found out she was adopted she asked the Stuttgart authorities if they knew anything about a cat medallion. Stuttgart wrote back and said there was a drawing of a cat in her records. It had been copied from a gold medallion found with the infant when she was adopted. Why do you ask about the cat, Alex?"

Alex fingered the cat medallion in his pocket. It was smooth and worn in his hand, all but the uncut jewel eyes. He hesitated only a moment, then pulled it out. "I found this medallion with the letters and the books. It must have belonged to the Baroness." There, that was truthful enough.

Joanna took the cat, compared it to the drawing on the letter and gave it back. "They look the same, don't they?"

Alex nodded as he stared out the window, trying to think. He didn't really register on what he saw, beer pouring out one of the kegs where someone hadn't turned off the tap, kids jumping in the pool fully dressed, three guys climbing up the barn roof.

"You know, if the Baron thought the Baroness's real mother was both Jewish and unmarried, it would be reason enough for him to kill her." Joanna's voice was intense. "A Nazi would do that, even to his own wife, believe me."

Yes, that was possible, but it didn't answer everything. It certainly didn't answer why Alex had been led to find Libertas Cottage or the closet full of Nazi material, or for that matter, these books and letters. Most of all, it didn't answer why Klaus had attacked and nearly killed him twice. One unseen force was leading him to discovery. Another unseen force was trying to stop him. No, Alex was sure there was more to the murder than the Baroness possibly having a Jewish mother and an unknown father. He was meant to find something . . . know something . . . do something . . .

Alex tapped his fingers on the books lying on the windowsill. Books. Two books. He'd forgotten about the second book, *Handbook for Everyday Law*. He picked it up. It had to be important too, or it wouldn't have been in the desk drawer with the medallion. As far as Alex was concerned, the section on divorce was the only one that might have any significance. Maybe when the Baroness found out her real mother had been killed by the Nazis, she had asked the Baron for a divorce and he had shot both her and himself. After all, with terminal cancer, the Baron had nothing to lose.

As Alex riffled through the book to find the chapter on divorce, a scrap of paper caught his eye. It was marking page 93, the chapter on wills. He had to be open to anything. This scrap of paper could be a signal too. He'd have to take the time to look the chapter over.

At first the words were a jumble, but then as he forced himself to concentrate, they began to make sense. Actually, drawing up a will was simple. All it took were two witnesses, both of them witnessing the other two signatures. The garbagemen. Alex had forgotten about them, but they had said they had witnessed a contract for the Baroness. She had paid them and told them not to come back. She must have been afraid they would tell the Baron what she'd done. And she'd probably written the contract in German so the garbagemen couldn't read it.

Wills . . . wills . . . a will was a contract, wasn't it? Dad had said the whole estate had been in the Baroness's name and Alex knew from what he'd found in the Baron's closet that she had willed everything to an American Nazi party. But why would she want to will her estate to Nazis after she found out Nazis had killed her real mother? She wouldn't, that's what.

Of course. That was it. A new will! That was what the garbagemen had witnessed. When the Baroness learned about her mother's death, she had written a new will. And Alex just bet the Baroness had been writing Dad to tell him about it when the Baron had shot her. That would explain the envelope Alex had found in the wastebasket addressed to his father at his law firm address.

Joanna grabbed Alex's arm. "You know something. What is it? You owe me."

Joanna was right. Alex did owe her. But he'd only tell her the facts. He didn't owe her anything beyond the facts. Someday maybe, but not now. "In her will, the Baroness left the Red Roof Farm estate to an American Nazi party. Right after the Baroness got this letter with the facts about her real mother, the Baron killed her. I think it had something to do with her writing a new will."

"A new will? So what does that mean?"

The party outside was in high gear. The whole house throbbed to the beat of the Innocent Bystanders and

Klaus was adding his own uproar of rage and frustration. It was almost dark and Bruce had turned on the floodlights. Kids were wandering in and out of the house. Most were in costume—cowboys, disco girls, bums, fright wigs, gorilla masks. Some had already been upstairs, and a scattering of red outfits and Nazi uniforms mingled with the other costumes. Alex saw it and yet he didn't see it. He had only one thing on his mind. That insulin bottle was nearly empty. Time had run out. He turned to Joanna.

"It means that will is important, and somehow I've got to find it."

...Twenty-two

Alex didn't know where to start looking. Not here in the den. The Baron's presence dominated the den and Alex couldn't imagine the Baroness hiding her will here. The kitchen. The kitchen, with its windows full of green and growing plants, belonged to the Baroness.

"Come on, Joanna, we'll try the kitchen first."

"The kitchen? Why not her bedroom?"

There was no way Alex could explain the special vibes he felt in the kitchen or how those plants had been flourishing independently of what he was or wasn't doing to them. "It's just a guess," he hedged.

Until he came out of the den, Alex hadn't realized how many people had already arrived at the party. Kids were milling around everywhere. Two couples in soaking-wet bathing suits were making out on the sofa. Spilled-over plastic cups of beer littered every table, and Alex knew the furniture was going to be stained with a mess of white rings. Someone had brought the Baron's portable TV downstairs and a whole crew was sprawled on the floor eating hot dogs and drinking beer while they watched a ball game.

Three girls dancing on the stair landing admired themselves in the mirror over the fireplace. As Alex and

Joanna pushed their way through the living room, two guys started down the bannister from the second floor on the seat of their pants. Zap! The rivets on their jeans scraped along the mahogany railing. Alex winced as both of them hit the landing with a crash and the three girls scattered out of their way, screaming.

"They're going to wreck this house just like I said." Joanna sounded furious.

"I know, I know. But we have to take care of this other business first." Alex would have to deal with the party later.

The kitchen was a worse scene than the living room. A cluster of kids was rummaging in the refrigerator and Alex saw one girl in a Roman toga eating cocktail onions. *His* onions. A mustard jar lay broken on the floor and a bright yellow trail led into the pantry where someone had walked through it.

"They're going to destroy this place, Alex," Joanna insisted.

"Okay, okay, drop it, will you?" Alex was so uptight, even Joanna was beginning to annoy him. If she complained one more time, he'd just have to tell her off.

"You don't have to yell at me," Joanna snapped. Beads of sweat glistened on her upper lip and tendrils of hair clung damply to her face. She was as jumpy as Alex as she yanked open the cabinet doors and began banging pots and pans around.

Like the house, the party and everything else, Alex would have to worry about Joanna later. He shouldered past some guys who were slicing up a ham and eating it straight. He couldn't let that bother him either. All he wanted right now was to find the will. He'd start with the plants. One had already fallen and lay smashed in a rubble of new green shoots, dirt and broken clay pieces. Alex kicked the mess aside and began his search. He lifted up every plant and checked under them, looked behind the curtains, along the windowsills, even in the watering can and under the bottles of plant fertilizer. It didn't take long, and he didn't come up with anything.

Now what? Alex stood by the window, looking around the room for another idea. Maybe he'd been wrong. Maybe the Baron had destroyed his wife's will after he had killed her. No, if that were so, why would Alex have been coaxed, urged, coerced by every means possible to find it? Alex dried his glasses with his handkerchief and mopped his sweaty face. He couldn't ever remember being hotter. He had to get fresh air before he exploded.

Without saying anything to Joanna, he raced through the back hall and out the door. Kids crowded the back stairs like birds lined up on telephone wires. One whole step was taken up by a guy either fast asleep or passed out. Stepping over him, Alex resisted the urge to boot him off into the bushes.

Fresh air. Alex breathed long and deep, but the air was so thickly hot it just clogged up his head. Or maybe that was the noise affecting it. The Innocent Bystanders were still at it, and here, with the loudspeakers directed right at him, the noise must have been eighty decibels. And Klaus hadn't let up his monotonous racket. All of a sudden Alex had a horrible thought. What if some kid unlocked Klaus's cage? Or what if someone or something, unseen and unknown, let Klaus out? It didn't matter how many kids were at the party, Klaus would head straight for Alex. Twice Klaus had done that, and twice he had come pretty close to finishing off Alex.

Alex could still call it quits and forget the whole thing. It was the safe way to go. He took a couple of tentative steps back toward the house.

"Hey, Alex, come here."

It was Sherrie calling to him. She sat at a card table in the driveway with a box of money in front of her. Someone had rigged up sawhorses across the driveway to cut off traffic, but the barriers had only served to force the cars onto the grass. Deep ruts scarred the lawn.

His mind still on Klaus, Alex walked slowly over to Sherrie and the short, husky young man who was with her. Sherrie had on one of the Baroness's red dressing gowns—open almost to the waist—and it was pretty impressive. She lit a cigarette and tossed the match on the ground.

"Bruce is looking for you, Alex. Oh, by the way, this is George Duffy. Alex Phillips." Sherrie smiled up at George and flashed her dimples.

So this was the famous George Duffy, Sherrie's ex-boyfriend. He didn't look like anything special. "Hi," Alex greeted him, then turned to Sherrie. "Those kids in there are tearing the house apart."

"We can clean up tomorrow. It's no big deal." Sherrie giggled. "I mean, this is the party of the century. And aren't those Innocent Bystanders unreal?"

"Yeah, unreal band, unreal party."

Alex's sarcasm was totally lost on Sherrie. "Does Joanna have those photographs of the Mercedes?" she asked. "That day we drove into town, George had the day off and he doesn't believe we have a $28,000 Mercedes to drive around in. And some idiot locked up the barn so I can't show him." Sherrie pointedly blew a lungful of smoke at Alex.

It was the smoke in the face that did it. Sure, Alex could back down on this whole thing, but then he was right back on Bruce and Sherrie's level where he'd been before. No, he had to see it through, scared or not. But first he had to get something to drink. Alex took the Kodak envelope of pictures from his pocket, handed them to Sherrie, and picked up a half can of beer someone had left on the table. It was warm, but he was so thirsty he didn't care. As he finished it off, he happened to glance at the three pictures of Libertas Cottage that Sherrie had separated from the rest and tossed to one side. Something about the top one caught his attention. It was the photograph that included both the sofa and the painting of the bird over it. It had bothered Alex when he first saw it, and it bothered him now.

Then, as he held it up to the glare of the floodlight, he realized what it was. His blue high school track shirt was sticking out from under the blanket on the sofa. It was right where he had found it the night Klaus had broken into the cottage. That meant this photograph had been taken *after* Alex had arrived at Red Roof Farm, *after* he had spent those first few nights in the cottage and left his track shirt behind. There was no other way the shirt could have been in the photograph. Alex hadn't taken the picture, and Bruce had never even been in the cottage until the night they'd found Klaus. How these images had been recorded on the film Alex didn't know. Or care. All he cared about was that the jigsaw puzzle with the random pieces had finally fit together.

Twenty-three...

Alex threw the photographs back on the table. The key, he needed the key. He raced back to the house, maneuvered around the bodies on the steps, rushed in the back door and into the laundry room where he'd hidden the keys. It only took him a second to find the one he wanted.

"Let me through. Coming through." Alex charged back down the stairs and took off across the yard at a run.

"Hey, Alex, Bruce wants you," Sherrie shouted after him.

Without answering, Alex wove his way through the shoulder to shoulder mob. Bruce and Sherrie had said a hundred people were coming. It seemed more like three hundred, and every one of them was shouting, yelling, dancing, laughing, drinking. The acrid odor from the charcoal grills mingled with cigarette smoke, the sweet smell of pot, car exhaust and hot bodies.

At least the Innocent Bystanders were taking a break. They were clustered around the beer kegs with everyone else. With the music stopped, Klaus's barking sounded wilder than ever and Alex could hear him crashing against his cage in a frenzy. It was a good sign that Alex was on the right track. And it was helpful too. No kid in his right mind would let a dog loose that was acting like that. As for Klaus getting out by any other means, Alex just wouldn't let himself think about that possibility.

For the first time since the party began, Alex saw Bruce. He was bent over adjusting one of the microphones. Dressed in jodphurs, boots and some kind of military jacket decorated with medals and ribbons, he looked like the Baron in some of his early photographs. He was even sporting a gun in his holster the same way Alex imagined the Baron had carried his gun.

Alex didn't linger. Right now he didn't want Bruce to spot him and nab him for some job or other. He ducked behind a gang of kids bouncing a girl trampoline-fashion on a blanket, and from there skirted around the side of the house to the front. As he made his way around the cars, vans, jeeps, pickups and motorcycles that were parked haphazardly all over the front lawn, he was so hot his shirt was as soaked as if it were raining. If only it would rain, it might cool things off. And cool off the party as well.

As soon as Alex was beyond the front yard, he picked up speed and headed down the driveway at a good steady pace.

"Alex, wait for me!"

It was Joanna. Alex turned without breaking his stride. Joanna pounded down the driveway behind him, her wrap-around skirt flying and her sandals clacking on the hardtop. Joanna. That was okay. In fact, that was just right. Alex slowed down enough for her to catch up to him.

"Hey, where do you think you're going without me?" she demanded. Her long legs matched Alex's pace. "George Duffy said you took off in this direction in a big hurry."

Alex grinned triumphantly. "I know where the will is."

"Where?"

"Not far from here."

Alex and Joanna had reached the woods. It was darker in here, cooler, damper, quieter. Klaus's barking sounded reassuringly remote, and even the renewed efforts of the Innocent Bystanders were diminished. They ran in a companionable silence for fifty yards or so when Alex smelled it. Smoke. Not exhaust smoke, charcoal smoke, cigarette or pot smoke either. Fire smoke. There was no mistaking it.

Joanna must have smelled it at the same time. "Fire!"

Alex didn't reply. He knew where that fire was and knew what it meant. He began to sprint and so did Joanna. They passed the traffic bump and came around the turn. In the wooded gloom, Libertas Cottage was only a shadowy outline. But it was the very darkness that accented the little fingers of flame licking around the window frames and the smoke lazily curling from under the eaves. They both stopped short.

"What is this place?" Joanna asked.

"The Baroness's cottage. It's where she hid her will." Alex was sure the will was in there and he had to get it.

"How could a fire start out here for no reason?"

"Probably spontaneous combustion. The place is full of paint and turps and oily rags." Maybe it was spontaneous combustion and maybe not. It also could have been a last-ditch, desperate effort to prevent Alex from finding the will. But there was no time to mull that over now. Alex peeled off his shirt and wrapped it around his face.

"Run back to the house, Joanna. Call the fire department. And hurry."

Joanna grabbed his arm. "You're not going in there. I won't let you."

"I have to."

"No!"

Alex yanked his arm away and pulled the cottage key from his pocket as he ran up the path. He had to get in there. The longer he waited, the worse the fire would get. He leaped onto the porch and unlocked the door. At least there was air circulating inside from where Klaus had broken the window. But the door was hot under his touch. Cautiously he eased it open.

The windowed end of the cottage was on fire. The curtains were ribbons of flame and the plants had disappeared behind a mantle of smoke. Little darting flames flickered around the edges of the rag rug and smoldered along the bottom of the sofa. Through the choking haze, Alex saw the painting of the bird still on the wall. So far it hadn't caught fire. And that painting was what he wanted. He knew it as surely as if the Baroness had told him.

"Alex, come out of there!"

Joanna was yelling at him from the porch. Why hadn't she gone for help like he'd asked her to? Alex wanted to shout at her to get going, but he didn't dare use precious air doing it. His lungs already ached.

Keep as close to the floor as possible. That was the first rule for fires. Alex would have to crawl across the room. He dropped on his hands and knees, thankful he had on jeans and not cut-offs. The floor was hot, but not unbearable. He pulled his shirt tighter around his face, resisting the temptation to take a deep breath. No, don't breathe at all. Like a soldier under fire, he got as low as he could and scrambled across the floor. He pulled himself up on the sofa, then tried to stand. But he was coughing and dizzy. He steadied himself on the back of the sofa. Now the whole room was enveloped in smoke. Don't panic. Lift the painting off the hook. But it wouldn't come. The wire was twisted around the nail. Alex ran his hand up under the painting to release it, but the wall was so hot he snatched his hand away. The fire must be ready to burst right through.

He'd have to cut the painting out of the frame. He reached in his pocket for his Swiss army knife, but all he found were his wallet and the Baroness's cat medallion. His fingers felt the sharp tip of the cat's pointed ears. He'd have to use that. But he had to hurry. His singed sneakers were beginning to smell and the heat was penetrating right through to the soles of his feet. Alex hopped up and down trying to cool them. Now it was getting hard to see. He pulled out the medallion, and with his left hand holding his right hand firm, he dug hard into the canvas, wielding the medallion like a knife. He heard the canvas rip as he worked his way around all four sides of the picture frame. Then the canvas fell out into his hand. Taped to the back of it was a sheet of white paper, typewritten, with signatures at the bottom. The will! It had to be.

Alex started to climb down from the sofa, but it was no good. The rug was completely on fire and the stench from the burning wool was suffocating. He'd have to jump. A standing long jump was all it was, Alex told himself. He'd done it countless times. Nevertheless, his hands were unsteady as he rolled up the canvas and jammed it in his back pocket. He felt lightheaded enough to pass out. But he couldn't pass out. He had to get out of here. Don't breathe. Just get going. He tensed every muscle in his body and prayed his legs would give him the thrust he needed. He leaped. Even as he soared through the air, he knew it was a good jump. He hit the edge of the rug, fell, then tumbled over and over. But he didn't reach the door. He'd have to crawl the rest of the way. It didn't work. He couldn't make it. His strength was gone. He felt himself beginning to lose consciousness as the searing heat in his lungs choked off the last of his air.

Dimly he was aware of someone pulling on his arms. His stomach scraped along the hot floor, across the porch, and bumped down the porch steps. He was on the hard ground. Someone was bending over him. A face pressed against his face. A mouth against his mouth. A sense of air coming in and out. A gradual awareness. Still, that mouth against his mouth. Air and more air. Alex opened his eyes, but the face was so close it was a jumble of features and hair. His breath came easier now. His lungs were clearer. He waved his hands to indicate he was all right. The mouth lifted off his mouth. The face move 1 and took shape. Hazel-brown eyes looked worried. Joanna.

Alex struggled to sit up. "I told you to get help." His voice was a hoarse whisper and his lungs still hurt.

"I flagged down a kid on a motorcycle and told him to phone from the house. I couldn't leave you." Joanna started to cry. Her face was filthy and smoke-smudged. "You could have been killed. You almost were killed."

Alex nodded. "Yes . . . except for you, maybe so . . ." There was no way to thank her that would cover the way he felt now. He'd thank her later when he could think more clearly and put his words in order.

Behind them Alex heard the crackle and snapping become a sucking roar. The old cottage was like kindling. The Stygian darkness of the woods was lit by the twisting, knotting flames. The cottage was going and there was no saving it. But Alex had the Baroness's will. He had done it. No, not just he. Joanna too. Alex pulled the painting from his pocket and handed it to her.

"It's the will." It still hurt to talk.

Joanna flipped her hair behind her ears the way she used to, but now that it was cut short, it fell back over her face. She took the painting, turned it over and held it up to the dancing light. It didn't take her long to read it.

"It's the will, all right. It's in German, and the Baroness wants Red Roof Farm and everything in it sold, with the money to be divided between Norrison County Memorial Hospital and the American Diabetes Association. She signed and dated it May twenty-eighth of this year. There are two other signatures that must be witnesses."

The witnesses were the garbagemen. And May 28 was the day before the Baroness was killed. She must have made out a new will as soon as she learned about her real mother dying in a concentration camp, then hidden it here in Libertas Cottage. She probably was about to write Dad and tell him about it when the Baron shot her.

If Alex expected any kind of reaction, spoken or unspoken, seen or unseen, he was mistaken. All he was aware of was the savage violence of the fire, and above his head, the tip-tap sound of beginning rain on the trees. A few cooling drops fell on his face. The weather had broken at last. Alex put his hand in his pocket for the comforting feel of the cat medallion but it wasn't there. He must have dropped it in the cottage. It no longer mattered. It had served its purpose.

Though the rain was coming down hard, the Innocent Bystanders, under the protection of the patio roof, were still at it. Most of the kids, who had chased after the fire engines to watch the firemen put out the last of the fire and soak down the surrounding trees as a precaution, had returned to the party and picked up right where they had left off. The rain wasn't clearing them out at all. It was reviving them.

Alex walked up to the patio, nudged aside the red-headed guitarist and shouted into the microphone. "Now hear this. Now hear this. The party is over. Finished. Get in your cars and go home." Alex was still coughing and hoarse but he knew everyone had heard him because they all turned around.

Bruce, down by the pool with Sherrie, looked up, then started across the yard at a run. His gun in its holster bounced against his hip.

"What do you think you're doing?" he yelled.

"I'm shutting down the party. Permanently."

Actually Alex was surprised to hear himself tell Bruce off that way. Joanna seemed surprised too. And Alex must have looked a little crazy as well, with his singed hair and filthy wet clothes that reeked of smoke. On second thought, telling Bruce off felt good. Alex leaned into the mike again.

"If you're not all out of here in twenty minutes I'm going to call the police."

Without even looking at Bruce, Alex took Joanna's hand and led her across the yard through the muttering, angry crowd toward the barn. As they approached the cages, they heard Klaus whining. But it wasn't the vicious whine of a killer, it was the mournful whine of a dog pleading to be free. As soon as Alex and Joanna rounded the corner, Klaus leapt against the wires, his tail wagging. Alex reached up to unlock the cage door.

Joanna pulled away. "Are you out of your mind?"

"Klaus is fine, I promise."

Alex opened the cage door and knelt down as Klaus ran to him. He worked his fingers deep into the thick fur behind Klaus's ears and scratched him. As Klaus nuzzled his face against Alex's shoulder, Alex knew for sure that Klaus was free of the Baron at last. That was what Alex had wanted for himself this summer, to be free and on his own. And he *was* free. But it had taken a lot of doing. He would never tell anyone what had happened. For that matter, he wasn't sure what had happened himself. The spirits of the Baron and Baroness pitted against each other with him as their pawn in the middle? Was that what it had all been about? Maybe someday he'd be able to make sense of it, but for now it was enough to know he had not only found the will, but had also seen the whole thing through without backing down.

Alex stood up, took Joanna's hand again and whistled at Klaus to follow. After what he and Klaus had been through, they belonged together, not just for now, but forever. He'd take Klaus home with him in the fall, was what he'd do. The three of them headed toward the house in the rain. The party was breaking up. People were leaving. The dark, secret Von Durst part of Alex's summer was over, and the open, shining Joanna part was about to begin.

ABOUT THE AUTHOR

JUDITH ST. GEORGE is a popular author of many mystery novels for young readers. Besides writing, she spends a large amount of time lecturing at school libraries and for teacher groups. Ms. St. George is a graduate of Smith College and lives in New Jersey with her husband and their four children.